*Praise*

"Maggie Shayne                                          ars!"
                                                    —Forster

# THE GINGERBREAD MAN

"Maggie Shayne beautifully combines a twisting plot with a thrilling romance. . . . The characters will steal your heart."     —*New York Times* bestselling author Lisa Gardner

"Shayne's haunting tale is intricately woven, and her quirky supporting characters . . . will capture the reader's sympathy."     —*Publishers Weekly*

# DESTINY

"Intense, mystical, and lyrical, this novel takes a pair of powerful witches torn apart by an ancient evil and brings them full circle back to love. One of romantic fantasy's most accomplished authors."     —*Library Journal*

# INFINITY

"[A] dark, enthralling brew of love, danger, and perilous fate."     —Jayne Ann Krentz

# ETERNITY

"A rich, sensual, and bewitching adventure of good vs. evil, with love as the prize."     —*Publishers Weekly*

"A hauntingly beautiful story of love that endures through time itself."     —Kay Hooper

# Immortality

## Maggie Shayne

JOVE BOOKS, NEW YORK

**THE BERKLEY PUBLISHING GROUP**
**Published by the Penguin Group**
**Penguin Group (USA) Inc.**
**375 Hudson Street, New York, New York 10014, USA**
Penguin Group (Canada), 90 Eglinton Avenue East, Suite 700, Toronto, Ontario M4P 2Y3, Canada
(a division of Pearson Penguin Canada Inc.)
Penguin Books Ltd., 80 Strand, London WC2R 0RL, England
Penguin Group Ireland, 25 St. Stephen's Green, Dublin 2, Ireland (a division of Penguin Books Ltd.)
Penguin Group (Australia), 250 Camberwell Road, Camberwell, Victoria 3124, Australia
(a division of Pearson Australia Group Pty. Ltd.)
Penguin Books India Pvt. Ltd., 11 Community Centre, Panchsheel Park, New Delhi—110 017, India
Penguin Group (NZ), Cnr. Airborne and Rosedale Roads, Albany, Auckland 1310, New Zealand
(a division of Pearson New Zealand Ltd.)
Penguin Books (South Africa) (Pty.) Ltd., 24 Sturdee Avenue, Rosebank, Johannesburg 2196,
South Africa

Penguin Books Ltd., Registered Offices: 80 Strand, London WC2R 0RL, England

This is a work of fiction. Names, characters, places, and incidents either are the product of the author's imagination or are used fictitiously, and any resemblance to actual persons, living or dead, business establishments, events, or locales is entirely coincidental.

IMMORTALITY

A Jove Book / published by arrangement with the author

PRINTING HISTORY
Jove mass-market edition / September 2005

"Immortality" was previously included as a short story in *Out of This World* published by Jove in August 2001.

ISBN: 0-515-14078-3

JOVE®
Jove Books are published by The Berkley Publishing Group,
a division of Penguin Group (USA) Inc.,
375 Hudson Street, New York, New York 10014.
JOVE is a registered trademark of Penguin Group (USA) Inc.
The "J" design is a trademark belonging to Penguin Group (USA) Inc.

PRINTED IN THE UNITED STATES OF AMERICA

10  9  8  7  6  5  4  3  2  1

# IMMORTALITY

# Prologue

*For the first time in four thousand years I was ready* to die. And it looked as if I would get my wish. For the flames surrounded me, searing my flesh, and every breath I drew burned in my throat and lungs. And yet I could see them. Beyond the smoke and dancing tongues of ravenous fire, I could see them. My husband, the man I had loved, and his mistress wrapped up tight in his arms, safe, outside, bathed in the cool night air while I roasted. Through the window glass I watched them, beyond the flaming draperies and through the thickening smoke—and then the window exploded, and the fire filled the open space. Even my preternatural eyesight couldn't pierce the wall of flames then.

It was over. He'd left me for dead, likely relieved to be rid of me. He would probably celebrate my demise.

*The hell he would.*

Something rose up in me. I was tired, tired of living, tired of fighting to stay alive, and tired of hating. I told myself to just close my eyes. Just lie there and let the hungry fire do its work. But something inside me fought back. It made me struggle to my feet, that insistent something. It forced me to drag myself through the inferno, toward what I sensed was the rear of the house. My dress caught fire. My hair smoldered and smoked, and my skin blistered. I would have screamed in anguish had I a voice, or even a breath left in me. But I didn't. If I'd been an ordinary woman, I'd have been dead at that point. But I wasn't ordinary. I wasn't mortal. So I stumbled onward, a living torch, and I tasted hell. Finally I fell, unable to go any farther.

But it was cool, damp ground beneath my body. It was blessed icy rain that pelted down on me from above. Life-giving rain.

And still that something inside, whatever it was, pushed me onward. Urged me irresistibly onward. I tried to get to my feet but couldn't rise even as far as my knees. So I dragged myself forward. I clawed my fingers into the wet soil, and I pulled myself inch by agonizing inch, onward. I suppose I couldn't bear the thought of *them* coming upon me this way. Seeing me with my skin charred black and my life force ebbing low. They would finish me off, if they found me.

Natum had taken everything from me. *Everything.* I wouldn't let his be the hand that took my life as well. No, I would die on my own terms.

And so I crawled . . . inched, toward the cliffs. "To hell with him," I whispered when at last I reached ahead of me to find there was no more ground to grasp. I opened my eyes and saw yawning darkness and far, far below, the boiling white froth of the sea. "To hell with both of them. And to hell with the world."

With one last effort, I, Queen Puabi, the darkest of the Dark Witches, pulled myself over the edge and into oblivion. And as I plummeted I wondered how many times I would drown and revive and drown again before my power ran out. And what would become of me then?

Could there be peace for one as purely evil as I? Or would I remain trapped in some semblance of awareness even while the sea creatures fed on my flesh? I didn't know. I didn't care.

*I didn't care.*

Anything was better than the anguish I left behind.

Or so I thought until I smashed through the surface of the sea, like smashing through concrete, and into its briny depths, which burned far more than the flames had done.

# 1

*He* thought his heart stopped cold when he saw the dead woman floating in the sea. At first he'd glimpsed only color and shape. Something white and oval hovering beneath the jewel-blue ripples of the ocean. He'd stopped rowing then and leaned over for a closer look. Her pale, lifeless face bobbed up, broke the surface.

"Jesus!" Matthew jerked away so fast he stumbled and fell, nearly tipping the small boat over. Then he sat there on the floor of his rowboat, stunned and gaping like the fish in his pail. His heart hammered. Squaring his shoulders, he got up onto the seat, slid to the side, and looked again.

She was still there, still dead, and she still looked startlingly like Gabriella. Dark, dark lashes rested eternally against her sculpted cheeks. Her lips were tinted blue and full, her nose, straight and small. Her arms were unclothed, hands delicate and lily white.

Water lapped over her face. Tiny waves, flinging themselves onto her lips, her eyes, as if in an effort to claim her.

Hell, he couldn't just leave her there.

Matthew told himself to buck up and do the right thing. If he had come to one conclusion during his temporary retreat from the world, it was that from now on, he would make an effort to do the right thing. So he would haul the dead beauty to his island, keep her there until the impending storm passed, and radio the authorities.

Sighing deeply, he knelt in the bottom of the small boat, leaned over, and managed to get hold of one of her arms. Then he frowned. She wasn't cold. Cool, yes. But not cold. He drew the woman closer, until he could get his hands beneath her shoulders, and then he pulled her up and inward. Her head cleared the boat's side and lolled backward. Her neck and shoulders were above the water level, and he bent to get a better grip, putting her face directly below his, upside down and void of expression. He did not like being this close to a dead person. He'd been spending far too much time contemplating death lately.

Suddenly the pale lips opened wide, and the dead woman sucked in a desperate, strangled breath. Her body arched backward so forcefully that he almost lost her to the sea. He was so startled by her sudden animation that he damn near let her go.

He rapidly regained his hold on her, tugging harder now that he realized he wasn't recovering a body but saving a life. God, he'd been so certain her chances were nil. Her eyes flew open, looking wild and dangerous, electric-blue— too vivid to be real, and flecked with gold—and she began to twist and struggle.

"No!" he barked. "Settle down, woman, or you'll drown yourself. I'm trying to save your life here."

She stilled instantly, maybe startled by his tone. It had startled him, too. He hadn't barked at anyone that way in almost three months. Hell, he'd probably scared her half to death, he thought. She seemed totally disoriented. He pulled her mostly nude body out of the water, into the boat, and she let him. Then she just lay there between the seats, water sluicing off her skin and her short, dark hair soaking his sneakers, his feet. Her clothes, what remained of them, were in tatters. Rags that might once have been a skirt clung to her from the waist down. From the waist up she was completely naked, and apparently unconcerned by it. She didn't try to cover herself. Then again, she'd nearly drowned. Having a stranger see her breasts was probably the least of her worries. And yet he did see, and he did notice. She was very cold. So it was tough not to notice.

She shivered, and he dragged his gaze away from her breasts.

"What do you want of me?" she whispered.

He narrowed his eyes on her, gave his head a shake, and started to peel his sweater off. As he pulled the sweater over his head, he caught the glint of sunlight on steel. Looking up fast, he saw her dainty, waterlogged hand clutching a deadly-looking blade—and bringing it down fast. He flung up an arm just in time to deflect hers. Then he caught her wrist in his hand, exerted pressure, and eyed the double-edged dagger she'd damn near plunged into his chest just now.

"Drop the knife, dammit!"

She shook her head, her eyes flashing with life, with anger, with violence, though only moments ago they'd been lifeless and dull. They were like lapis stones, her eyes.

"Crush my wrist," she all but growled. "Go ahead, mortal, and see how fast it heals again."

He stared at her, and wondered how someone could look so much like Gabriella and yet be so completely different. This woman personified rage. "You're delirious. Put the knife down before you make me hurt you."

She shook her head. Matthew squeezed her slender wrist in his hand until she cried out in pain and the blade clattered to the bottom of the boat. He eased his grip, set her down again. She slumped against the side of the rowboat, looking at her wrist as if confused.

"I'm weak," she muttered. Then she closed her eyes tiredly. "You should have left me in the sea."

"You try anything like that again, I'll throw you right back in."

Those blue eyes opened, and she glared up at him.

He glared back. Then he bent to pick up her blade, looked it over. It was a nice piece. If the stones embedded in the handle were real, it was worth some money, too. "I'll just hang on to this for you," he told her, tucking it into his belt. Then he retrieved his sweater from the seat where he'd dropped it and handed it to her. "Put this on."

She looked at him with fury in her eyes. But she took the sweater and pulled it over her head, thrust her arms into the sleeves. "Where are you taking me?"

He nodded at the tiny island in the distance. "There."

"And what is there?"

"Nothing much, besides my villa. It's a private island. *My* private island." He sat facing her and bent to the oars. He saw the way she looked toward the west. On a clear day, the ghostly shape of St. John's would be visible in the distance. Saba was closer, and you could almost always see its distinctive volcano-shaped cone, but not today. It was far from clear in the distance today. "There's not time to go any farther," he told her, and nodded toward the darkness far in the distance. "Storm coming."

She narrowed her eyes on him in suspicion.

"What, you think I'm lying? That I *want* a psychopathic drowned rat in my only haven? Trust me, lady, I'd take you to one of the big islands if I could. But I can't, so unless you think you can swim that far in a storm, you're stuck with me."

He thought those laser-blue eyes would burn him, they grew so fiery. "If you think I am *stuck* anywhere, you are sadly mistaken." Then she leaned back in the boat, closed her eyes, and there was not another sound from her.

He wasn't sure if she'd passed out, died, or was just ignoring him. He rowed faster. It didn't take long before he was out of the boat, tugging its nose up onto the sandy shore of the small island. Then he scooped her up and saw with relief that she was still breathing. She was light in his arms, limp in them, her body leaning into his chest as he carried her inland, over the sand to harder ground and then along the barely discernible path through the palms and tropical plants, to his home away from home. It wasn't much, his island villa. Not compared to his seaside mansion back home. But it served him well when he needed to escape. And he had needed that. Badly.

It was as if the fates didn't *want* him to escape, though. How else could he explain what had happened here just now? Finding this woman—a woman who, aside from her vivid blue eyes, could have been his wife's evil twin.

What the hell did it all mean? Who was she? And why would she want to drive her pretty dagger into her rescuer's heart?

\* \* \*

*Puabi woke to softness and a surrounding warmth that* had worked its way into her body. She opened her eyes with a start, her fingers curling, clawlike, into the surface on which she lay. She'd expected water. Water had been her entire world for so long . . .

But that man had pulled her from the sea.

Sighing, she eased her grip on the mattress beneath her, tried to focus her vision, and took stock. She was alive. But far from strong. Her head still pounded. Her lungs ached. Her skin and eyes burned and felt raw. This tiredness clung to her, and her vision wasn't good even by mortal standards. It was blurred and dull.

The room around her seemed bright, sunny. She made out windows, and rich dark wood furnishings. A fire danced warmly in a freestanding fireplace. And the bed in which she lay was huge and soft. Fit for a queen, she thought, almost smiling at the irony.

"Awake, are you?"

She turned her head slowly and saw the man sitting in a rocking chair near the bed. He set aside the book he'd been reading and leaned forward, elbows resting on his knees. He was a big man. Broad-shouldered. Very dark. His skin bronzed by the sun, and his hair as black as her own. He had the thick, dark brows of a Sumerian, but aside from that she could make out little of his face.

"How are you feeling?"

"Why do you want to know?" Her voice emerged rusty with disuse.

He got to his feet, poured water into a glass, and offered it to her.

Puabi blinked at the large, blurred hand that held the glass.

"You're dehydrated," he said. "You should drink all you can stand."

She had never liked being told what to do. She liked it even less when the man doing the telling was correct. Sitting up with no small effort, she accepted the glass, tipped it to her lips and drank. She drained it, despite his protests, which began halfway through, then set the glass down. The cool water hit her stomach like a brick. For a moment she thought the liquid might come back up, but she quelled the sick feeling with a hand to her belly and slowly lay back onto the pillows.

"Probably a little at a time would have been better," he said. "Your stomach's been empty for a long time."

"How would you know that?" she asked, her eyes falling closed.

"Your hair is like straw, your skin is burned from the sun and chapped from the salt water. Your eyes are so bloodshot I'd be surprised if you could see straight."

"I can't."

He sighed and set the glass aside. "How long were you in the water?"

There was something about his voice. Its deep timbre had a controlled quality to it. As if he were keeping it level only with great effort. And there was something else, something that tickled her nerve endings with a static charge.

"I don't know," she answered.

"How did you get there?"

She opened her eyes to look at him, but as before, he was unclear. Dark hair, longer than was fashionable in men of consequence today. And he was one of those, she knew that much. He'd called this his island. He spoke with an air of authority and command. And something else. Pain.

He was waiting for her answer, she realized. She didn't give him one.

"There must have been a fire," he said. "What remained of your clothes had been burned."

"I don't want to talk about that."

He blinked slowly. She couldn't make out his eyes, but she knew they were focused on her face, and she felt their intensity. "Then you do remember."

"I remember. I wish I didn't. Either way, it's no concern of yours."

"You're right, it's not." He shrugged as if he could care less about her trauma. "There's a lukewarm bath waiting for you in the next room. Soak in it for a while. It'll soothe your skin."

Puabi tilted her head to one side and frowned at him. "I don't . . . understand."

"A little oatmeal in the water," he said. "An old trick my

father taught me. Good for everything from sunburn to poison ivy." She thought he might have smiled slightly, but sensed it wasn't a real smile. "Go ahead," he said. "Take your time." He started toward the door, then paused, turning back. "Uh . . . there's a bell on the nightstand to your left. Take it with you into the bathroom, just in case."

She blinked through her swimming vision as he left her alone. What was he up to, she wondered. Why was he bothering with her comfort? Bringing her water, running her bath? She got to her feet, but her head swam with dizziness. Gods, things were not right. Not with her—and even more clearly, not with the mortal. He was up to something. She felt it right to her bones.

# 2

*Puabi lay in the cool, soothing water, head tipped back,* eyes closed. The mortal had been right—though his actions were suspect. In her experience no man was this kind without some hidden motive. Still, whatever he'd put into the water did ease her burned skin. But her eyes . . .

She lifted a soft washcloth, dripping wet, and laid it gently over her closed eyes. No doubt the salty seawater had done some harm. But her body ought to have healed itself by now. It was taking an unreasonably long time. Ah, but then again, she had died and revived countless times at the whim of the sea. Her power must be waning very low indeed. And there was only one way to restore it, to prolong this hideous existence. To find another Immortal High Witch—one of the Light Ones—and kill her.

The idea held little appeal, oddly enough. And the mortal had taken her dagger. That did not bode well, and only added to her suspicions about him.

Sighing, she dunked her head beneath the water to rinse away the conditioner that had been soaking in her hair for several minutes now. She'd had all she could bear of lying up to her neck in water, after so many days surrounded by the stuff. Tiredly, her muscles protesting in pain, she got to her feet, stepped out of the tub, and used a thick soft towel to gently dab herself dry. Then she rubbed her hair down as well.

Her vision was still blurred, but it was slightly clearer than before. She could see more of the room's details. The tub was freestanding and claw-footed. The walls and ceiling were white, and bamboo mats were scattered around on the floor. Large, arching windows let sunlight flood the place, and she glanced through one of them for a moment. She glimpsed palm trees, blue sky, a sandy beach with waves lapping at it. Then the brilliance hurt too much, and she had to look away.

Hadn't the mortal claimed there was some horrendous storm looming? That yellow sunlight didn't look stormy to her.

So she'd caught him in a lie already. That confirmed her opinion that he was up to no good.

Sighing, she continued her inspection of the room. Aside from the porcelain fixtures, everything in the room was rattan—from the cabinets on the walls to the towel racks to the frame around the full-length mirror. She paused there and squinted at her hazy reflection. Her skin was still an angry red color. Tender to the touch, and warm. Her hair stuck up like black feathers, but it felt softer than before. Slinging the towel over her shoulder, she found a comb lying on a stand and pulled it through the short black layers.

"Everything all right?" His voice came from beyond the door, and again the sound of it made her skin prickle with some kind of awareness.

Looking toward the door, she noticed a large white article of clothing hanging from a hook there. "Fine. I'll only be a moment." She dropped the towel to the floor and went to retrieve the white clothing, which turned out to be a large cotton robe. Its touch was cool and delicious on her skin as she pulled it over her arms, around her waist, and tied the sash. It hung well below her knees. From what she could tell, she was decently covered—not that she particularly cared, but she was in no shape to gut the mortal should he try to assault her, driven to violent lust by a glimpse of her flesh. It wouldn't be the first time, she mused. She opened the door and stepped back into the bedroom.

And she smelled food. Her stomach growled loudly even

as her eyes sought the source. There, beside the bed, was a
tray that emitted aromatic steam. The man stood near it. She
sent him a suspicious look. "Why are you being kind to me?"
she asked him.

"This isn't kindness," he said slowly. "It's decency. I'd do
as much for a stray dog."

"And likely get your hand bit off for your trouble," she
snapped, even as she walked quickly forward and climbed
onto the bed, curling her legs beneath her and reaching for
the tray of food. Drawing it into her lap, she leaned over it
and sniffed. She smelled meat, vegetables, seasoning, toasted
bread, melted butter, cheeses.

"How are the eyes?"

"Fine," she lied as she moved her hands around on the
tray trying to identify the items. There was a bowl, and hot
liquid. Soup. And a small plate held some kind of a sandwich. And a cup . . .

"Careful, the tea's hot," he warned.

She ignored him, picking up the sandwich and bringing it
to her mouth. Grilled cheese. It was far from the finest meal
she'd eaten in her lifetime, but she thought she enjoyed it as
if it were. The soup turned out to be chicken broth with
noodles, vegetables, and hunks of meat. She devoured the
entire sandwich and drained every last drop of the soup. Then
as she lifted the mug of tea, the man took the tray from her
lap.

She looked up quickly, having nearly forgotten his pres-
ence. It was unusual for her to let her guard down with a
stranger—especially one who had taken her dagger and lied
to her in order to keep her here.

He set the tray aside. "I have some eyedrops here. They
might help."

She shook her head, not trusting him. "I don't need them."
Instead she sipped the tea.

"All right." He sighed and took a seat in the chair beside
the bed. "So why don't you tell me who you are?"

"I am Puabi."

She could see well enough to know when he tipped his
head to one side. "Just Puabi?"

"No, not *just* Puabi. Queen Puabi. I am of royal blood."

The flash of white told her he smiled. "Queen, eh? And what are you queen of?"

She averted her poorly functioning eyes. "A land that no longer exists. A world that is no more." Slowly, she closed her eyes. "You think I'm insane, no doubt."

"I didn't say that."

She took a fortifying sip of tea, but truly her head was feeling heavy on her shoulders. "Where am I?" she asked him, suddenly overwhelmed with the urge to go home, even though she knew there was no such place. She wouldn't recognize Sumer now. It was buried beneath the sands of four thousand years. New civilizations had covered over her own. They called it Iraq now, and it was peopled by children of Muhammad, not of Inanna.

"You're near the Virgin Islands. Roughly between St. John's and St. Kitts. The nearest inhabited island to us is called Saba. It's just five square miles—but it has a small airfield and a medical clinic."

She swallowed the lump that had formed in her throat. "I went into the Atlantic off the coast of Maine. I emerged in the Caribbean, in the tropics. Gods, how long must such a journey have taken?"

He was silent for a moment. When he spoke, he spoke softly. "I think you're still a little . . . disoriented."

"I came through the Triangle, didn't I?"

"The Bermuda Triangle? Yes . . . I suppose you could have."

"Perhaps that's got something to do with the way I feel."

"And how do you feel?"

She shook her head, searching for words. "I don't know. Odd. Different." She lifted her chin. "I want to leave here," she demanded. "I want to go to the mainland. The States. Now, today." She set the teacup on the nightstand, but it landed so near the edge that it toppled to the floor. She ignored the sound of the porcelain shattering, turned in the bed, and swung her legs to the floor.

"You can't leave yet," he told her.

"I can, and I will." She surged to her feet. Dizziness welled up like a tidal wave in her head, and her knees dissolved. Arms came around her, strong, fast, and firm. And there was something—some moment of déjà vu. A sense of odd, niggling familiarity about the man, even as he held her against his powerful body.

"Gods," she whispered. "Something is wrong with me. I feel . . . so strange."

"A few days in the sea will have that effect on a person," he said, and he lowered her carefully to the bed again.

"It's not that. It's more than that." She squinted up at his face, hovering over hers. "I know you," she whispered, the words dripping with accusation. "Who are you?" Why the hell wouldn't her eyes focus and allow her to see his face? She would know it. She was certain she would.

"Easy, Puabi. Come on, take it easy." His hand still cradled the back of her head, lowering it to the pillow before moving away.

"I want to leave," she said, but the words came weakly, softly.

"You can't. Not until the storm passes."

"There is no storm. You lie."

"I don't lie. There's a tropical storm stalled a hundred miles out to sea," he said. "The longer it sits there, the stronger it becomes. It could start moving in at any time, and I don't intend to be caught out there in a small boat when it does."

She let her eyes fall closed. It made her head hurt to strain them so hard in the effort to see him. "Then tell me your name. For I know we've met before."

"My name is Matthew. And we've never met. You're not the kind of woman a man would forget."

*And that was all. She was out cold.*

Matthew stared down at her, shaking his head in complete bewilderment. Who the hell was she? And just how much brain damage had she suffered? He sat on the edge of the bed, threaded his fingers into her hair, and probed her scalp. He took his time, felt every bit of it, but found no sign of head injury. That didn't mean much, though. The sun, the heat, the dehydration—she could have suffered a stroke or some kind of mental breakdown. Any number of things could be causing her delusions.

First she'd tried to kill him. Then she'd claimed to be a queen. And now she thought she knew him.

Hell, she certainly played the part of royalty well. She hadn't so much as thanked him for the food. Or for saving her life, for that matter. And a glance at the condition of the bathroom—towels on the floor amid puddles of water, tub still full—suggested she expected to be waited on.

But that wasn't fair, was it? She wasn't exactly in peak condition right now.

Asleep, it was stunning how much she looked like Gabriella. Awake, she couldn't have been more different. And the last thing he needed here was her face reminding him of his wife. Sweet, shy, lonely little Gabriella. She'd been lost. She'd foolishly thought he was her salvation. She said she loved him. And died because of it.

Hell. He closed his eyes, fought the regret that rose up. Gabriella was gone. The woman in the bed had nothing to do with his young wife. The resemblance was a coincidence. And she, Puabi, was a mystery. One he didn't need or want to solve.

Sighing, he reached for the bottle of eyedrops and leaned over her. With his thumb, he pulled one eyelid upward. "Trust me on this, your highness." He squeezed a few drops into her eye, then repeated the process on the other side. "I want you off my island just as badly you do."

Her eyes flew open and rolled back into her head. She thrashed, her arms flailing wildly. The lamp on the nightstand flew. Then she hit the stand itself, toppling it. She twisted and arched on the bed as he tried to catch hold of her, keep her still. God, she was burning up with fever. It had come out of nowhere. She kicked, then sat up, and though he tried, he couldn't hold her to the bed. How the hell could she be that strong? When she flung herself backward again, she slammed her head into the headboard. One hand slashed across his face and then raked her own chest. Trails of bright red blood beaded on her pale skin in the wake of her clawlike nails and trickled downward.

My God, she was strong! And she was hurting herself. She was like a wildcat, lashing out, convulsing, and he was damned if he knew what to do to keep her from harming them both. He caught one flying arm, then the other, and held on while she thrashed. He could only pray that she would wear herself out soon.

# 3

When Puabi woke again, she moaned softly and arched her back in pleasure even before she opened her eyes. She was lying facedown in the warm, downy-soft bed, and something cool and wonderful was stroking her back. Over and over, it moved soothingly, leaving blessed relief in its wake.

Then her mind cleared, her memory returned. She tried to roll over, even while reaching for a blanket to cover herself as she realized she was naked and fully exposed. But her hands didn't move. Frowning, she lifted her head, and tugged at the soft strips of cloth that bound her wrists to the headboard above her.

"You *dare* . . ."

"What, now you're complaining?" he said in that rich, velvet tone that stroked every nerve ending to life.

She couldn't see him. Could only hear his voice, and feel his hands smoothing something creamy and cool over her flesh. "A few seconds ago you were damn near purring."

"Take your hands off me," she commanded, and even to her own ears, the order lacked any real power.

"In a minute. Your skin is so burned it's blistered in places. This stuff will help."

"I don't want your help."

"You're not exactly in any condition to know *what* you

want. Much less what's good for you, so I've taken the decision out of your hands."

His hands smoothed a path over her buttocks. Cool, clinical, so soothing she wanted to sigh in relief. She twisted away from his touch, but she couldn't go far. "I knew you couldn't be trusted," she seethed. "I knew you were up to something."

"The only thing I'm up to is keeping you from killing yourself, or me, or both of us."

His hands moved down the backs of her thighs, spreading that coolness to the creases behind her knees, and lower, over her calves.

She relaxed in spite of herself. "I reacted the way I did when you pulled me from the sea out of sheer instinct. If you'd lived the life I have, you'd have done the same. And it's moot, anyway, because you took my dagger from me. I'm no threat to you now."

"Somehow I doubt that." He was massaging her feet, gently working the salve, or whatever it was, into them. But he stopped, and moved into her line of vision, and then he knelt beside the bed, looked her in the eye, and pointed to his face. Red scratches marred it. "You did this without any help from your fancy knife."

She flinched when he said it. She hadn't meant to. Her vision was significantly clearer than it had been earlier, and suddenly she wished it wasn't. "I did that?" she whispered hoarsely.

"Is that remorse I see in those strange eyes of yours, Puabi?"

She frowned at him, but she was no longer looking at his neck. Instead she'd turned her vision inward, searching her mind, her self, for the source of this uncommon emotion. "Yes," she said. "I think it may be. Incredible."

Blinking, she focused on his face, seeing it more clearly now than before. Brown eyes, hard eyes. Lines at the corners, small ones, frown lines. Wide jaw. Lips and nose both full. Sensual. By the Gods, he was handsome.

"You sound incredulous that you're capable of feeling sorry for having attacked me."

She nodded. "I am. Why should I be sorry? Your injuries

are minor, so why should even the slightest remorse plague me?"

His brows rose as one. "Maybe . . . because I saved your life?"

"You underestimate me. I was still a long way from dead when you found me. Though I suppose I might have expired, eventually, had you not."

He studied her, shaking his head. "Here I thought the big question was why you'd want to kill me after I took you in, fed you, tried to help you . . ."

"I told you, instinct. I've had to fight to stay alive for a very long time. It's my nature to attack before the attacker has the chance. Strike fast, strike first, live to strike again."

"That's a pretty brutal philosophy." Then he tilted his head. "Actually, it sounds a lot like my own."

"Really?"

He nodded. "Yes. Really. Until recently."

"Then you've changed your mind? Why?"

He averted his eyes as she searched them, and she knew she had hit on something sensitive—some tender spot. He was vulnerable there. It was good to know a man's weakness early on.

"Roll over. The ointment's pretty well soaked in on this side."

Pursing her lips, she thought about refusing. She considered snapping the bonds that held her, which she was certain she could manage with minimal effort, even in her weakened state. The one thing she could be certain of, however, was that her back felt a great deal better than before, while the front of her still burned and stung as if she'd been dragged naked over sandpaper. The man hadn't tried anything inappropriate yet. If he did, she would kill him. Perhaps. Or perhaps not. It wasn't a complicated matter at all.

She rolled over, the strip of cloth that held her wrists twisting easily.

The man went still, his gaze sliding slowly down her body, lingering where it shouldn't, heating with desire.

"Look your fill and let's get on with this, shall we?"

He let his eyes slide up her, from her toes to her eyes. "Pretty full of yourself, aren't you?"

"You're the one who tied me up and stripped off my robe."

"*My* robe," he corrected. "And I only tied your hands because you went wild on me. Look at your chest."

She lifted her head from the pillows and saw the marks she'd dug across her own chest. "Point taken. But just why am I bound now, Matthew Fairchild?"

He frowned at her. "How did you know my last name?"

"I assume you told me."

"I didn't."

She frowned in thought, but quickly dismissed the question with a shake of her head. "I'm in significant pain, mortal. Would you apply your lotion already?"

He nodded, reached for the cloth that bound her wrists. She shook her head. "Leave it."

His eyes flew to hers, flaring slightly.

She met his gaze without blinking.

"I'm not into playing bondage games."

"Oh, come now. Have you ever tried?" She taunted him with her eyes. Then she shrugged. "Besides, I can pull free of your little knots easily. Remind me to show you sometime how to properly restrain a subject."

Matthew shook his head and kept his eyes averted. As if he thought she might not see the animal desire in them that way. Much less the guilt that came with it. She did, though. She saw it all. He might be an amusing distraction, this handsome mortal.

He sat on the edge of the bed, and dipped his fingers into the jar on the nightstand, and they came out dripping with a clear, gel-like substance. He moved his hand toward her, and she stiffened in anticipation. The cold stuff touched her heated skin, her shoulder, and slowly he smoothed it down her arm.

"What is it?" she asked.

"Aloe, mostly. It's working wonders on your back already."

"I'm a fast healer," she said softly, her eyes riveted on his hand as he dipped it into the jar, drew it out again, and spread more of the stuff over her neck, and then gently upward, following the line of her jaw, sliding over her chin. His fingers moved against her face, her cheeks. She closed her eyes, and he touched her forehead, her nose, the bit of skin above her lip. There was something in his touch . . .

His hand was trembling.

The moment she noticed it, he drew it away, and she opened her eyes to look at him. "What is it?"

He shook his head, but there was pain in his eyes. "You . . . remind me of someone," he said at last. Then the emotional look left him, and the more cynical one returned to his eyes. "At least you do when you aren't bitching at me or trying to kill me."

She tilted her head, ignoring his barb. "Who?"

"No one." He coated his fingers again and returned to his work, spreading the stuff over her other arm, all the way to her wrist, skipping only the part covered by the strip of cloth. He moved on to her hands, her fingertips, which he did one by one. Then he went to the foot of the bed, and started at her ankles, smearing ointment up her shins, over her knees, and along her thighs. He didn't shy away when he neared their juncture. He kept going, painting her pelvic bones, hips, lower abdomen. He only skipped the dark curls. Then he was at her waist, her belly. Her rib cage and sides. His hands worked some kind of magic, soothing away her pain and leaving a cold fire in their wake. His touch felt good. Like the caress of a lover. And she was too much a woman not to be aroused by it.

He took his hand away, gathered more aloe from the jar. Came back. She couldn't help it. As his hand neared her breast, she closed her eyes in anticipation. And then that coolness touched her, and she let her breath whisper out of her. As his fingers neared the center, she knew her nipples hardened expectantly. She didn't care. And then his fingers were there, softly, gently rubbing the cold gel over her nipple. Too soon they moved away. But he began again at the other breast, and she thought she would die if he didn't touch her more thoroughly. When he got to the nipple this time, a soft cry was wrenched from her. His hand stilled, fingers on her hard nipple. She arched her back to press herself against his touch, and he responded with gentle pressure. Too gentle. And then he swore softly and moved his hand away.

"Don't stop," she whispered. She opened her eyes, met his, and saw a flicker of desire in his velvet-brown gaze. "You may take me if you like."

His eyes flared wider, slid down her body again, and he licked his lips.

"It's been a very long time since a man's touch has felt the way yours does," she whispered. "We're both adults, Matthew."

He turned his head away from her, forcing his eyes elsewhere. "As I said before, you're in no condition to know what you want right now."

She set her jaw, and with a deep growl, tore free of the fabric that bound her wrists. "To hell with you, then."

He looked back quickly, eyes sharp on her. She thought he expected another attack. But what kind, she wondered. Was she afraid she would kill him or ravage him? Then she looked at his eyes, and she knew he wasn't afraid. Not at all. He stood there expectantly, watching her, and waiting. Fully ready to deal with whatever she might attempt to do.

She narrowed her eyes on him. "This woman I remind you of," she said softly. "She was your lover?"

"She was my wife."

"And you wronged her in some way?" she asked, certain that he had. It was the only explanation for his having shown any tendency at all toward kindness to her—the only reason he hadn't throttled her by now, or tossed her back into the sea where he'd found her. And the only reason he hadn't taken her up on her offer of sex. Guilt. She could smell it on him.

He was stone silent for a long moment, and then, his face stark, he said, "I killed her."

# 4

*Night fell, and the strange woman slept. He sat in a* chair beside the bed and wondered what the hell he was going to do with her. She didn't look *exactly* like Gabriella, he mused as he studied her face. In fact, the more time he spent with her, the more different she seemed. Gabriella had been fragile, and frail. She'd been clingy and dependent. She'd been hollow and empty inside. She'd been quiet and shy.

Puabi was the opposite in every way. She was fire to Gabriella's ice. She was technicolor to Gabriella's pastel. She was aggression, and sexuality and danger.

Hell, the two women looked less alike by the second.

*She dreamed. She hadn't dreamed in so long, she couldn't* even remember the last time. She'd thought once, that perhaps when one became immortal, one lost the ability to dream. But she'd never been sure.

The dream was not a good one. She was floating, tossed up and sucked down by the icy sea. Gods, she was so cold. It was as if she would never be warm again. And it was getting colder. She spun, caught as if in a whirlpool, sucked deeper and deeper into the frigid hubs of the sea. And then she was floating there, freely floating, not struggling to breathe. The water looked like sky. The fish, like stars, and she was no longer certain where she was. Around her, she saw other forms floating. Faint, misty shapes, some more distinct than others. And she wondered who they were.

*Souls.* The word whispered in her mind. *I'm in the Hall of Souls.*

Blinking, she tried to see them more closely, but this damn blurred vision wouldn't allow it. She realized she was in the Devil's Triangle. And somehow, she was seeing things that were not real.

*But they are real,* that voice said in her mind. And she realized suddenly it was not her own voice. Not some inner knowing. It was coming from without.

"It's not real," she cried aloud, but her words were only bubbles in the waters. "I don't have a soul."

*You gave it up, Puabi. You gave it up when you made yourself into one of the Dark Ones. But now you'll have the chance to get it back again.*

"How?" she asked, breathless, desperate, close to death.

*You have a mission, Puabi. A job to do.*

"What?"

Suddenly she was being pulled upward again, spiraling back to the surface before she'd received her answer. "No! No, not yet! Not yet! You have to tell me what I have to do! What am I supposed to do?"

"All right, all right, it's okay."

"No, no, no." She was shaking, freezing, shivering so hard her teeth chattered. And then he was beside her, around her, holding her to him. Gods, he was strong, and warm. His chest was firm and his arms powerful. He wouldn't let her fall into that cold sea again. He wouldn't.

Slowly his warmth seeped into her, and she stopped shivering. But his arms never eased their grip. "I loved you so much once. Why couldn't you love me?" she whispered, her voice weak, breaking. "All I ever wanted was for you to love me."

She felt him stiffen against her, and for a moment she wondered if she was speaking to Natum or to the stranger, Matthew. But it made no sense. She'd never loved Matthew. She snuggled closer and fell into a deep, dreamless sleep.

Once she heard him speak to her softly, but she couldn't respond. "Who the hell are you?" he whispered. "Where did you come from?"

When Puabi woke, there was sienna-colored light infusing the place with a muted glow. She studied it, wondering why she felt there was something she had to do today. A ... mission. Something ... there had been a dream ... or was it a memory?

Warmth, heaviness, against her and around her.

Matthew.

She rolled over carefully. The man, the stranger who had pulled her from the very mouth of death, was holding her close to him. He lay on his side, facing her now, his mouth only inches from hers. His legs were entwined with hers, and his arms held her close. It was as if she were his beloved.

She almost laughed, a bitterness welling up in her belly. To think that she could ever be that important to anyone. It had taken her more than forty lifetimes to finally figure it out. No one would ever love her. And why in hell would they? She closed her eyes as the memories of the things she had done came crashing in upon her like waves on the shore.

Why? What the hell was the matter with her? After all this time, had she suddenly developed a conscience? Gods, it made no sense! What was happening to her?

Lips touched her mouth. Lightly, very softly. A hand gently cupped her head, fingers sinking into her hair. His mouth was warm, and moist, and tender as it tasted hers. Oh, God, it felt good to be kissed by a man this way. She parted her lips and kissed him back. His arms tightened around her, and she slid hers around his waist, hands splayed on his muscular back. The kiss deepened then, as he came slowly awake. He moaned, and his tongue slid into her mouth to taste deeply, as if she were some luscious confection that he craved. He licked at her mouth, suckled her tongue, fed on her lips, and she relished every second of it.

And then he drew away and opened his eyes. Fiery eyes, passion-filled. His voice gruff, tense, he whispered, "Tell me your name."

"Puabi," she said. "I'm Puabi."

He nodded, closing his eyes slowly. Then he rolled over and sat up in the bed, lowering his feet to the floor, holding his head in his hands. "You said something last night. In your sleep. You said, 'Why couldn't you love me?' "

She closed her eyes. "I don't know why I even care."

His head came up slowly, but he didn't face her. "About who?"

Swallowing hard, sensing he had a reason for asking that went beyond anything obvious, she saw no harm in speaking of it, even though she recalled feeling confusion at the time—naturally there was only one man she could have been speaking to in her troubled sleep. "My husband. Natum—Nathan is the name he uses now. He never loved me. Every time I needed him, he was with his lover. When I lost our child, when I was left for dead in that burning house, when I was swept away by the sea. All he could think of was her."

Matthew turned slowly, a look of pain etched on his hard face. "You lost a child."

She lowered her head. "A son. Stillborn." Her heart constricted. "It destroyed me."

"I'm sorry. And . . . sorry about your husband, too."

"Don't be. I've wasted far too much time fighting for a man who never wanted me."

"You deserve better."

She closed her eyes. "I deserve exactly what I got. You don't know me, Matthew. I'm . . . evil."

He looked down at her, his eyes intense—she didn't have a clue as to why he always seemed so intense when he looked at her. But it wasn't the first time she had noticed it. "He did that to you, and you think you're the one who's evil?"

"You don't know the whole of it."

"I don't want to know the whole of it," he said, walking to a chair and picking up some clothes she hadn't seen before. A pair of shorts with a drawstring and an oversized tank top. He handed them to her. "Do you feel up to breakfast?" he asked, changing the subject.

She nodded, sitting up in the bed. "The more I eat, the faster I'll mend."

He let his eyes move down her body, and a frown darkened his brow. "You mend any faster and I'll wonder if you're even human."

She glanced down at her chest, where he was looking. The scratches she'd put there herself were completely healed. And her skin looked as smooth as a newborn's.

"Yesterday you were burned so badly you were blistered. Today your skin looks as if it's never even seen the sun."

Puabi shrugged. "Who knew aloe was so powerful?"

She felt his eyes on her, probing, so she forced herself to meet his steady gaze head-on. He knew she wasn't telling him something. And she knew he knew it. "Matthew—there are things about me that you are better off not knowing. For now, suffice it to say that I'm not like other women."

"I'd figured that much out, Poppy."

She lifted her eyes to his. "Why do you call me that?"

Matthew shrugged, getting to his feet. "Puabi is a mouthful. Poppy—suits you. Beautiful. Deadly. Mysterious. Occasionally mind-boggling and quite possibly addictive." He said it playfully, teasingly, but there was a serious undertone to his words.

He inclined his head and led the way out of the room. She quickly pulled on the makeshift clothing he'd brought to her and followed him, relieved that he didn't push her for any more information.

The living area of the villa was huge, and took up most of the front of the place. Wicker furniture was scattered sparsely in the high-ceilinged rooms beneath giant fans that spun in perpetual slow motion. The place was not all that large or fancy, but you could feel the money behind it all the same. It took wealth to make a place look this casual. This comfortable. This effortless.

"The kitchen's this way," he said. "What would you like for breakfast?"

"What do you have?"

"Everything," he said, leading her through to a smaller room equipped with spotless white appliances. Marble tiles lined the walls and the floor. "I had a full supply flown in so I wouldn't have to leave until I was ready."

She narrowed her eyes on him. "Just how long have you been out here?"

He looked away. "Two, almost three months."

"Alone? All this time?"

His shrug pretended to be careless. "For the most part."

"Why?"

He didn't answer her. "Bacon and eggs sound good?"

"Sounds fine."

He nodded and turned to the refrigerator. Left with nothing to do but wait, Puabi wandered back into the living room, and then she caught sight of something so surprising that she made some sound of alarm without meaning to.

Matthew came to her, asking what was wrong. Then he followed her gaze to the photograph that hung on the wall and swore softly. "I'm sorry. I forgot it was there," he said.

"My God, who is she?"

Drawing a breath, he sighed deeply. "Gabriella. My wife."

Puabi stepped closer, eyes riveted. "She could be my twin. No wonder you look at me the way you do." Turning to him, she saw the pain in his face, in his eyes. "You loved her very much."

"No," he said. "I should have loved her. But I didn't. And she died because of it."

Frowning, she tilted her head to one side. "She's the reason you're out here, hiding away from the world? Because you should have loved her, and didn't? How could that kill a person?" Then she blinked slowly. "Was it suicide, Matthew?"

He met her eyes and she knew she was right. "I'm not a good person, Poppy. I'll tell you that much. I'm a bastard, to be honest. A lot like your own husband, I imagine, which makes it even more ironic that you ended up here. Only in my case, it wasn't another woman I preferred over my own wife. It was my business, and my freedom."

She shook her head. "I don't believe you. My husband was relieved by my death—or, my presumed death. You . . . you've exiled yourself from life to come here and grieve for her. It's not the same at all."

"No? Well, she's just as dead, Poppy. And so is the child she was carrying." He spun on his heel and returned to the kitchen.

Puabi let him go, her knees trembling so much she had to sit down in a big wicker chair before she fell down. Her gaze was drawn irresistibly back to the photograph of the woman who was her mirror image except that her eyes were black as night. Ebony eyes that, for a moment, seemed to stare right back at her. "Gabriella," she whispered. "A child. Gods, a child." Her own pain, old, but so very sharp still, cut again into her heart and clutched tight in her barren womb. Nothing had ever hurt her so much as losing her baby, so long ago. Nothing ever would. It had been the end for her. Part of her had died with her tiny stillborn son.

Gabriella's face was softer than Puabi's. The lines of jaw and cheekbone, less harsh and drawn. And her eyes were jet, while Puabi's were blue with flecks of gold.

Puabi stared at her, anger rising up. "You're nothing like me," she whispered. "I'd have given anything to save my child. If you were anything like me you couldn't possibly have taken yours with you into death."

Pans banged in the kitchen, and Puabi looked that way. Matthew was hiding here, punishing himself for not loving his wife. How could he blame himself for that? You couldn't force yourself to feel something that simply wasn't there.

She lowered her head, bit her lip. By the Gods, neither could Natum.

*Oh, what the hell is this? I'm feeling sorry for Natum now? I'm pitying him and understanding why he wronged me so? What the hell is this?*

Why couldn't she have stayed the way she was? Hating, raging against everything and everyone, acting without conscience or consequence, despising her husband and his lover for betraying her. It had served her well for more than four thousand years. Why should it begin to change now?

One thing was sure. No matter how many deaths Matthew Fairchild claimed—he couldn't come close to the blood that stained her hands.

Smells reached her from the kitchen. Coffee. Bacon. They made her stomach growl. Then there was something else that distracted her from those smells. A sound, like a deep, droning buzz, that grew louder. She rushed to the window and looked out to see a small yellow airplane descending on the island.

# 5

"What the hell is she thinking?" Matthew hurried to the doorway when he heard the familiar sound of the pontoon plane's motors. Poppy was there ahead of him.

"Who is it?" She looked nervous.

He opened the door impatiently.

"Matthew, give me my dagger."

Frowning, he looked at her. "You expecting some kind of attack, Poppy?"

Licking her lips, she averted her eyes. "You never know."

He took her hand in his and started for the door. They were outside and halfway down the path by the time he realized he was still holding it. It had been an impulse, grabbing her hand that way. It had been automatic. And it still felt right, her small hand in his. He stopped walking, looked down at their joined hands, then at her face.

She met his eyes briefly. Something unspoken moved between them, some palpable, electrical charge. And he didn't know what the hell it was, but he decided not to let go. Then her eyes seemed to shutter themselves, as if in defense, and she tugged her hand free. "I'm not Gabriella," she told him.

"I know that."

"Do you?"

He felt his lips quirk upward at the corners. Not a smile,

but close to one. "If you'd ever met her, you wouldn't ask, Poppy."

"It's Puabi."

She was still damned bristly. Almost hostile. He had yet to figure out why, but then again, he hadn't figured out anything about her. How she managed to heal at the speed of sound being at the top of the list. And now was not the time. He turned and continued to lead the way. The path was a winding one, shaded by palms even on the brightest days. This was not one of those. It was damned ominous outside today. Still. Utterly still, with that odd heaviness to the brick-tinted atmosphere.

They emerged from the trees near the horseshoe-shaped inlet where the yellow pontoon plane was just now skiing to a halt. He stopped where he was and waited for the engines to shut down, the hatch to open. Finally, Murial hopped out onto the pontoon nearest her. She reached up to close the hatch, then turned and stepped off the floating ski and onto the sand.

Matthew waved and moved toward her, and when she caught sight of him she waved back, but then she froze, her hand in midair, her eyes fixed on a spot beyond him.

He glanced sideways, but Puabi wasn't there. She'd stopped walking a few steps back and stood now staring at Murial.

"What's wrong?" he asked. "Come on, it's all right. She's a friend of mine."

Poppy met his eyes. "A friend?"

He nodded. "Murial works for me. Has for years. I'd trust her with my life."

Her eyes narrowed on his. "And I suppose you think that means I ought to trust her with mine?"

"Come on, Poppy. Look at her." Murial was willowy, pale, and with her ready smile not at all menacing or frightening.

Puabi breathed slowly. She still seemed exceedingly wary. "All right, then. If you trust her."

"I do." He started forward again, and this time she came with him. When they reached the point where Murial stood, they found her gaping. Murial was tall and slender as a reed, with long, perfectly straight blond hair and the sun-kissed face of a girl half her age. Pale lashes and brows, light blue eyes, a killer smile. She wasn't smiling now, though. She looked stunned, and Matthew felt a twinge in his gut. He should've left Poppy behind at the villa, so he could have prepared Murial for her appearance.

"It's okay, Murial," he said softly. Waves lapped against the pontoons, making slapping sounds. Other than that there was dead silence.

"But . . . but how . . . how could she . . . ?"

He reached out and clasped Murial's hands in his. "This is Puabi," he said. "Not Gabriella. Although I understand your reaction. Mine was pretty much the same."

The woman frowned, her eyes dragging themselves away from Puabi to meet his. "My God, the resemblance is . . . but what's she doing here, Matthew?"

"I'm stranded here," Puabi answered. Matthew knew by her tone, regal and impatient, that she resented Murial's asking him instead of her. "Until the storm passes."

Murial looked at her, studied her, her gaze intense.

"Exactly," Matthew said. "And speaking of the storm, what the hell were you thinking coming out here today, Murial? Do you know what a risk you're taking?"

She seemed to shake herself out of her inspection of Puabi. "I come out with the weekly reports every Friday."

"But the storm could have kicked up while you were in the air."

"It didn't," she replied.

"It wasn't worth the risk."

She rolled her eyes. "You're as overprotective as always, I see." Then she slipped her arms around him, hugged him gently. "How are you, Matthew?"

"Better," he said. And he glanced at Poppy and realized he wasn't lying about it. He'd given Murial the same reply every Friday for more than two months now, and this was the first time it had actually been true.

Poppy had something to do with that. He wasn't sure what. Maybe she'd just given him something else to think about besides his own guilt. Right now, though, Poppy looked even bitchier than usual.

Murial released him, and he said, "Let's get you back to the house. We were just about to have some breakfast."

"Great. You know I never turn down a meal."

You wouldn't know it to look at her, he thought idly. "Murial is my executive assistant," he told Poppy as they headed back along the path to the villa. "But she's more than that, too. Frankly, I don't know how I'd have made it through the last few months without her." He shook his head slowly. "I couldn't have left the business to anyone else. I'd have had to stay myself."

"Are you sure that would have been a bad thing?" Puabi asked.

Her tone startled him, and he shot her a look. "I needed to get away, to grieve in private, and try to heal. It was Murial who made me see that, and by stepping in for me, she gave me the means to do it."

Puabi sent Murial a saccharine smile. "You must be a very kind and generous soul."

Murial's expression was just as sweet, though more genuine, Matthew thought. "I care a great deal about Matthew."

"And Gabriella, no doubt," Puabi put in.

Murial nodded. "I was her best friend."

Puabi glanced pointedly at Murial's hand, which was on Matthew's shoulder, and said, "I can see that."

Whoa, what the hell was up here? He could feel the tension emanating from Puabi, and she was definitely firing rounds at Murial, but he wasn't sure why. He picked up the pace, and the two women kept up.

"I apologize for staring at you back there," Murial said after a moment. "You look so much like her—I thought I was seeing a ghost at first."

"Real people are far more frightening than ghosts," Puabi replied, and the words had an undertone that was almost threatening.

Back at the villa, the moment Murial went into the bathroom to wash up, Matthew took Puabi by the arm and drew her into the kitchen, closing the door behind them.

"You don't like her," he said. "Why?"

"I don't like anyone," she responded.

"You like me."

Her gaze raked him. "You're confused, Matthew. I have a compelling urge to have every imaginable form of sex with you. Repeatedly. That does not mean I like you."

His throat was suddenly very dry. To have her put it so bluntly . . . hell.

Poppy smiled wickedly at him. "I've rendered you speechless?"

He shook his head and tried not to visualize her words quite so clearly in his mind. But for a moment all he could see was a vision of tangled, sweaty limbs, and moist lips, and . . . hell. "I just want to know why you took such an instant dislike to Murial." He frowned then as a thought occurred to him. "Is it . . . jealousy?"

She tipped her head to one side. "I suppose it could be some form of that. But if it is, it's based on simple animal instincts. I haven't had my fill of you yet, so I resent the competition of another female." She seemed to mull that over for a moment. "Yes, that could be it."

He closed his eyes. "Murial is not interested in me in that way. Gabriella was never the least bit threatened by her."

"Gabriella was a naive, trusting, needy little girl."

He frowned, hard. "How do you know that?"

Blinking, Puabi looked at the floor and shook her head. "I'm not sure. I just do. I knew it as soon as I saw her photo." Lifting her eyes, she said, "Am I right?"

"Yes. About Gabriella, at least."

"About Murial, too. I don't know what she wants from you, Matthew. Whether it's the same thing I do or not. But regardless, she wants something. And whatever it is, she's not telling you. I dislike games and hidden motivations. I prefer people who say what they mean and mean what they say. Even an honest enemy is preferable to a dishonest ally."

He turned away from her, faced the food that was even now cooling in its pans on the stove. "You're honest, I'll give you that." He reached to the cupboard over his head, and took three plates down, then turned and handed them to her. "Here, put these on the table, will you?"

She lifted her brows, looking down at the plates with disdain.

"Oh, come on, don't give me the royalty routine. You're obviously feeling better. So pull your weight." He put the plates in her hands, and as she carried them out of the room, he tried very hard to erase the images she had painted in his mind. She wasn't delirious anymore. She wasn't sick or fe-

verish or in shock. And she openly admitted to wanting to—
how had she put it?—have every imaginable form of sex
with him. Repeatedly. But she didn't like him.

Hell, did he really care? He didn't like her all that much
either.

*The lovely, lithe Murial spent most of the morning en-*
sconced in a sitting room with Matthew, on the pretense of
discussing business. Puabi listened at the door a few times,
and each time she did, that was precisely what they were
doing. Discussing business.

Maybe she'd been wrong about the woman. Murial
seemed kind, concerned. She spoke softly, smiled easily.

But how was she, Puabi, to believe she could be mistaken
about the woman? She'd been the ruler of Ur, most powerful
city-state of Sumer. She did not make mistakes.

She used the time when she was left alone to snoop
through Matthew's villa, where he had come to lick his
wounds after his young wife's death. At Murial's urging,
Puabi reminded herself. Interesting. It wasn't a large house,
but every inch was spotless, neat, organized. No television
or radio anywhere to be found, other than the shortwave radio she located in a small room in the back. She couldn't
have operated the thing if she'd wanted to, and had no interest in it anyway. What did interest her were the items she
found in the bottommost drawer of the stand on which the
radio rested.

Inside were things she knew instinctively had belonged to
the dead Gabriella. Photographs of her with Matthew on their
wedding day. Clippings announcing the marriage. A dark,
blurry ultrasound printout, showing the tiny pollywog-shaped
fetus she had carried.

Something hot stabbed at Puabi's belly.

At the very bottom of the drawer there was a diary.

Puabi reached for it, then hesitated, her hand hovering a
hairsbreadth from the tiny book. She glanced behind her, into
the hallway, but no sounds reached her. Matthew was still
occupied with Murial. She would have time.

She picked the diary up, opened it, and began to read. And
very soon, she was engrossed. All sense of time deserted her

as she fell into the pages, because the story that unfolded on those pages could easily have been her own. The only difference was that Gabriella had grieved while Puabi had raged. Gabriella had given up where Puabi had fought. Gabriella, in the end, turned her pain inward. Puabi had turned hers outward, unleashing it on everyone she encountered.

As she closed the book, Puabi was stunned to feel dampness flooding her eyes. She lifted a hand, touched her fingertip to her cheek, and drew them away staring in disbelief at the teardrop she had caught. She was even more stunned to hear Matthew's deep voice from the doorway, saying softly, sadly, "So now you know."

# 6

*She looked up quickly, no doubt startled to have been* caught red-handed with his most private possessions. No matter. It seemed perfectly logical to Matthew that Puabi would find and read Gabriella's diary. He felt almost as if he'd expected it.

What he hadn't expected was to see tears on her face.

She dashed them away with an angry swipe of her hand and got to her feet. "I'm sorry. I . . . couldn't help myself."

He nodded. "I didn't think any sad story would be enough to melt that hard, practical heart of yours, Poppy. But it looks like Gabriella's did."

She shook her head slowly, then turned and tucked the book back into the drawer. "Not her story. Mine."

"Yours?"

She faced him again, sliding the drawer closed. "Almost word for word."

He glanced behind him, into the hallway. He'd left Murial in the study, where she'd been making notes of his instructions for the coming week. She would be busy for a moment. And this was a side of the mysterious Puabi that he hadn't yet seen. He wanted to probe it—in private. He closed the door softly, then turned to face her again, and he said, "Tell me."

She shook her head slowly.

"Come on, Poppy, you owe me. You violated my privacy. You read my dead wife's most intimate thoughts. You know my worst secrets. Now tell me yours."

He saw her face change, saw the capitulation there. He hadn't expected that either, not without more persuasion than he had yet applied. Maybe . . . maybe she needed to talk it out as much as he needed to hear it.

He watched her sink back into the chair where she'd been sitting. Her eyes focused not on his, but on some spot beyond the wall. "You already know most of it," she said, her tone gruff. "My story is Gabriella's. I married a man as a matter of convenience. Although in my case, unlike Gabriella's, it wasn't a one-night stand or an accidental pregnancy. It was a treaty between nations. But the results were the same. I fell in love. He didn't. Not with me, at least. And it wasn't enough for me."

He nodded, not moving from his spot, afraid to jar her out of this revealing mood. "He was a fool, then. As much a fool as I was."

"No, Matthew. He couldn't force himself to feel something he didn't. No more than you could. I see that now. I just . . . I don't know why I didn't see it then." She drew her focus back in, from wherever it had been. She looked at him now. And her eyes were clear and sharp. "I think what pushed me beyond the edge of my endurance was the day I lost our son. He was stillborn while my husband was out searching for his mistress. I just couldn't forgive him. After that, hating came easily to me. I made it my life's work, in fact."

Sighing deeply, Matthew moved toward her, unable to stop himself. He reached down to brush a tear from her cheek with his thumb. "I'm sorry, Poppy. Losing a child—that's a hurt no one should ever have to know."

"On that we agree."

"Obviously the outcome was different for you than for Gabriella. You're still alive."

She nodded. "For now."

"What's that supposed to mean?" He tried to search her face, but she lowered her head. Matthew dropped to one knee and pushed her hair aside, trying to read her.

She refused to look at him, and changed the subject. "Gabriella's response to rejection was despair. Mine was rage. I lashed out against them—my husband, his lover. In the end, they escaped unscathed and my rage rebounded like a boomerang, coming back to harm only me. The house burned. I was trapped inside, and they left me there, left me for dead."

"How did you manage to escape?" he asked, his gut churning because he sensed that every word she spoke was true.

She shook her head. "I don't know. Something in me made me keep fighting. I dragged myself out of the fire, to the cliffs, and fell into the sea. I honestly didn't expect I'd ever emerge again. Not alive." Looking deeply into his eyes, she said, "And the rest you know."

He nodded slowly. Then he swallowed hard and decided to say what he was thinking. She'd been bluntly honest with him, after all. "It . . . has crossed my mind that you didn't end up here by accident. That maybe you're . . . some kind of chance at redemption for me."

"*Me?* Your *redemption?*" She smiled bitterly. "No, Matthew."

"I couldn't save Gabriella. But I could save you."

She shook her head again. "By saving my life, you cursed humankind to suffer my existence a bit longer."

"Don't say that, Poppy. It's bullshit and you know it. You're no more evil than I am."

She looked as if she were about to argue, but stopped herself. "Tell me what happened to Gabriella. I feel . . . I feel as if I know her, somehow."

Drawing a breath, he sighed deeply, rose to his feet. He couldn't get through this if he had to look her in the face. Instead, he paced a few steps away as he spoke. "It was a one-night stand. She worked in the mail room, and she caught my eye. I had too much to drink one night and . . ." He sighed. "She got pregnant. I married her. I said it was because of a takeover in progress with a Christian book publisher whose owners placed a high value on morality. But, hell, it wasn't that. There was something about her that just— I don't know—drew me." Looking at the floor, he paused for a moment. "I didn't intend to, but I became . . . fond of her. She was such a tender thing. So needy. She took my kindness for more than it was and began to imagine a happy ending for us. We'd agreed to a quiet divorce once the child was born. I'd promised her a generous settlement. She knew I would provide for her and the baby. I thought it would be enough."

"And it wasn't," Puabi said.

Having reached the far end of the room, he turned. "No. It wasn't enough. She confessed her love for me one night, told me she didn't want to go through with the plan. I was shocked . . . I reacted badly. Reminded her she'd signed an agreement."

Puabi closed her eyes, gave a little sigh.

"I know, I know. She was furious. We argued, and she took the car and left. I was going to go after her, but Murial called with a business emergency. She convinced me to give Gabriella time to calm down, and talk to her later, when we were both more settled."

"But later never came."

He met Poppy's eyes. "No. She drove the car off the road and over an embankment. It plunged eighty feet to the ground. The gas tank exploded and . . ." He looked at the floor as the memory of what had remained of his naive little wife floated through his mind.

Puabi came to him, and her hands curled over his shoulders. Her breath fanned his face when she spoke. "I'm sorry, Matthew."

"So am I. Sorry I wasted so much time. I could have had a devoted wife who loved me unconditionally. I could have had my child, safe and healthy and wonderful. Instead, I have my precious freedom and my all-important business." Lifting his head, he met her eyes. "And I don't give a damn about either of them anymore."

Their gazes locked. He saw the pain in hers, and recognized it. Knowing its source made it even more powerful to him. And she drew him suddenly, like a magnet. He leaned nearer. Her eyes fell closed, those thick lashes caressing her cheeks. And her lips parted expectantly. He closed his hands on her waist and bent his head. His mouth brushed over hers, and he could feel her breath on his lips.

"Matthew?" a voice called.

Jerking his head up quickly, he glanced toward the door. Then he looked at Poppy. She lowered her head and turned her back on him. One hand was pressed to her forehead, the other, braced on the nearby table.

"Are you all right?"

She nodded, but didn't face him.

"Poppy, what is it?" He clasped her shoulders from behind, felt them trembling just slightly. Was this a reaction to that almost kiss? It seemed like far more.

She stiffened her spine and turned to face him with a smile painted on her face. "I'm fine."

The door opened. Murial stood there, looking from one of them to the other with innocently curious blue eyes.

"I'm ready to head back," Murial said. "See you next Friday?"

Matthew turned, forced his attention on his friend. "Oh, no, you're not."

Murial frowned at him. "What do you—"

"You're staying right here, Murial. It's already late enough that you'd be flying in the dark, and that storm could easily hit before morning. I'm going to have to insist that you stay. And when you do go back . . . Poppy and I will be hitching a ride."

Murial's eyes flared wider. "You . . . but, Matthew, you aren't ready."

"I wasn't." He looked at Poppy and she met his eyes. "I think maybe I am now. Either way, it's time."

*Puabi wasn't sure what brought on the rush of weakness* that nearly put her on her knees when Matthew had been about to kiss her. Or what brought on the other feelings. Feelings that were utterly foreign to her. Her heart had twisted for Gabriella. And she'd felt Matthew's pain as well. Why? How could she feel for him when he'd treated his wife almost exactly the way her own husband had treated her? And when she'd anticipated his kiss, it hadn't been animal hunger alone burning in her. It had been something more. Something she . . . and her kind . . . did not feel. Were incapable of feeling—or so she had always believed.

The rush of dizziness that had followed, though, that was physical. Her legs had turned to water, her stomach had knotted up, and she would have fallen if she hadn't had the table for support.

Whatever it was, it passed quickly enough. But it left her weak and shaken. And wondering just how much life remained in her. If she suffered another mortal death—would she revive again? Or had she used every life she had ever stolen, during her endless months at sea?

They sat outside that night. Despite the storm so nearby, the sky was clear, and stars dotted it everywhere. Matthew had suggested a walk along the beach, since Puabi hadn't seen much of the island yet, and so the three of them walked barefoot in the sand between the shore and the villa. It honestly was beautiful here, Puabi thought. Like a small, lush oasis in a vast desert. Only the desert was sea.

"What's that?" she asked, pointing to a charred circle in the sand.

"They used to build bonfires there, I think."

"They?"

"The people I bought the island from."

"But you never have?" Puabi asked.

Murial clapped a hand over her own mouth to stifle a bark of laughter, but it escaped anyway. Matthew looked at her. "What?"

"Just the image of you, Mr. Tycoon, building a bonfire . . ." She shrugged. "Then again, I wouldn't have pictured you walking barefoot in the sand, either."

"No. Neither would I a short while ago."

Murial's smile turned softer. "This place is good for you, Matthew. It's healing you, I can see it."

"And I have you to thank for that."

A twinge of something that might have been jealousy nipped at Puabi's gut when Matthew reached out a hand to touch Murial's face. But it was brief. He dropped his hand to his side again quickly and said, "Let's build a fire."

"You're kidding," Murial said, and she shot Puabi a smiling look of disbelief. "He's kidding, isn't he?"

"Sit, both of you. I'll do the honors."

Puabi shrugged and looked around, spotting a hollow log that looked as if it had served as a bench in times past. She walked to it and sat, surprised when Murial sat on the other end. Matthew hurried into the woods, and came back moments later with an armload of twigs, dried leaves, and other debris. Then he vanished again, and returned with more sticks, larger ones. He arranged the kindling as carefully as if he were building a bridge, then headed back for more wood.

"A few weeks ago, I was afraid he would never bounce back," Murial said softly.

"It's like you said—the island is good for him."

Murial tilted her head to one side. "Maybe you're what's good for him."

Blinking in surprise, Puabi searched the woman's face. "I'm surprised to hear you say that."

"Why?"

A soft breeze kicked in from the sea, and Murial's blond locks danced in its touch. Puabi studied her face and saw nothing sinister there. "I guess I thought . . . you might have some romantic interest in him yourself."

"No, Puabi. I don't. I work for him. And I care for him, but only as a friend. Obviously, though, things are different between the two of you."

Puabi shook her head. "They can't be."

"Why not?" Murial asked.

Looking out toward the sea, Puabi was silent for a moment. The moon was just rising now, far out over the distant edge of the water. It sent silver ripples toward them. "There are reasons," she said at last.

Murial sighed, nodding to herself. "Puabi, you care about him. I can see that much." Puabi met the woman's eyes, but didn't reply. "Try to talk him into spending just a little more time out here. You don't know what he was like before. I was afraid for his life, I truly was. He'll listen to you. He needs more time. He's not ready to face those memories—not yet."

Before she could reply, Matthew was back, carrying logs this time. He arranged them near the fire and finally searched his pockets for a match. Murial got to her feet and offered him a lighter.

"Always prepared for anything," he said. "Aren't you?"

"I try to be," she told him.

Matthew knelt down and lit the fire.

# 7

$P$uabi was in Matthew's bed. She'd realized that only today. It was where he'd put her that first night, and where she'd been ever since, despite the fact that there was a guest room in the house. She knew there was, because that was where Murial was spending the night. Matthew had taken the sofa. She wondered about that. His putting her in his own room that first night, rather than the guest room. What did it mean? Or did it mean anything at all?

*Better question,* she thought, suddenly scowling into the darkness, *why the hell do I care?* She was not the sort of woman who spent her time musing over a man's motivations. Then again, she wasn't an empathic sort, either, most of the time. But there was no question she was feeling empathy for Matthew's suffering, and for that of the ill-fated Gabriella. Gods, Gabriella. She couldn't seem to go five minutes without thinking of the woman, seeing her in her mind's eye, like a younger, sweeter, innocent version of herself. Like a little sister.

"Sickening," she muttered, rolling over and punching the pillow into a more comfortable shape. And her mind was so occupied with all of these new and inexplicable feelings, that she was sure she was missing something else. Something vital. Her powers were weak, yes, but not gone. She sensed something afoot here. Unseen forces were stirring in the astral. Magick was at work. She could feel it, almost taste it in the air. But she couldn't identify it or pinpoint its source, much less its intent or nature. It was more an inkling on her part. A static charge and a whisper she couldn't quite hear.

What did it all mean?

She tossed and turned for hours, and when she finally did begin to drift off, it was only to be shaken awake again by that ghostly memory—or was it a vision? She was in the water, and the water turned to sky, and someone had spoken to her in a voice that sounded like her own—told her she had a mission, a job to do.

Sitting up in bed, shivering and sweating at once, she pressed her hand to her forehead, closed her eyes on hot tears. "What is it?" she whispered. Gods, her stomach was churning, her head awash in questions. "What the hell am I supposed to be doing?"

But no answer came. She listened, looked for signs, and heard only the soft whisper of the wind on palm fronds outside, and the occasional cry of a night bird.

Sighing, she flung the covers aside, and rose from the bed naked, warm, welcoming the kiss of that dark breeze coming in through the open windows. A walk, she thought idly. To clear her head. She pulled on Matthew's white cotton robe, cinched the sash at her waist, and padded quietly out of the bedroom and through the villa. She tiptoed through the living room, careful not to disturb Matthew, who she assumed was curled beneath the mound of blankets on the sofa. The door didn't squeak when she pulled it open, thank goodness. And then she was outside.

Closing her eyes, she hurried away from the house, along the path through the lush growth. Most of the plants were foreign to her. She heard scurrying in the brush and wondered what sorts of animals dwelled here. And then she didn't care. She emerged on the beach and stood there for a long time where the waves washed in, lapping around her ankles, covering her feet, muddying the sand that oozed between her toes. The breeze here was stiffer, cooler, invigorating somehow. She found herself closing her eyes, opening her arms to it. As if in response it blew harder, buffeting her body, tousling her hair. It was damp, that wind. It kissed her face with moisture, tasted of salt and seawater.

"What am I doing here?" she whispered. Opening her eyes, she searched the distance, the dark sea, and the black velvet sky. Its starry face was streaked with dark, clawlike fingers of cloud. "I don't understand."

"Maybe you're not supposed to."

The voice, soft and deep, came from very close to her, and she didn't need to turn to recognize it. Matthew's hands curled around her waist, and he drew her backward until her body pressed to his. "Maybe it doesn't matter."

Her head tipped back against his shoulder, and he bent his, so his lips touched her neck lightly, softly, then lingered there.

"There's some reason, Matthew," she whispered. "You were right about that. None of this is coincidence, and I should know . . ."

His whiskers rasped over her sensitive skin, and she sucked in a breath.

"Right now," he said. "There's only right now. This moment. What came before, what comes later, those things don't exist."

"But they do—"

"Not if we say they don't. Try, Poppy. We deserve this moment. We need it."

She did try. She felt the waves wash over her feet, and as they retreated, she imagined them taking time itself away with them. Her past, her crimes, the blood that stained her hands, all washed out to sea. Yes. Gods, yes, to be free of all of it.

She broke away from Matthew, running forward until the depth stopped her. The white robe dragged, wet and heavy, and still she moved forward, dragging her legs through the cooling water, deeper and deeper. The water reached her chest, and a wave broke over her head, soaking her and driving her to her knees. Then it surged back, lifting her, tugging her into its embrace.

But there were other hands. Human hands. Matthew's hands and his arms locked around her. His body melded tight to hers, and his mouth claimed hers. The tide washed back out to sea without her. She was anchored to him. And he was carrying her toward the shore, carrying her in his arms, kissing her, and there was nothing else. There was only here and now. This moment, just as he had said.

She clung to him, tasted the seawater in his kiss, and more. Her fingers tangled in his wet hair as he dropped to his knees in the sand. Still kissing her, he laid her down, and stared down at her hungrily, eyes blazing, as he untied the sash and flung the robe open wide. Then he bent over her and drank every drop of seawater from her skin, kissing her dry. It seemed to Puabi that his lips left fire in their wake, heating her flesh beyond endurance.

Then rising above her, he looked deeply into her eyes. "Don't love me," he said. "I don't deserve to be loved. I destroy what loves me."

"Don't love me," she told him in return. "I destroy all that I touch. And I will break your heart in the end if you let me."

He held her eyes for a long moment, and when he kissed her again, any hint of restraint washed away in with the waves that ebbed and flowed around them. Puabi pushed at his jeans, until he helped her to strip them away. And then he bent over her, nursing at her breasts, one, then the other. She arched toward him as his mouth moved over her body, in a useless effort to quench the fires he'd ignited in her skin, her belly, her thighs. And when he tasted more of her, she twisted her fingers into his hair and held on. The wet sand was cool beneath her back. The water washed over them in an ever more urgent rush. His hot mouth, demanding and hungry, fed at her. Pressing her wider, he delved inside with his tongue, sucking at her as if she were a ripe fruit oozing juices he craved. He pinched gently, deliciously, with his teeth, as if he could squeeze out more, then lapped up every drop, and demanded more.

She screamed aloud when she came, and her entire body shuddered with the force of her climax. And even then, he was sliding his wet, warm body up over hers, higher, covering her, spreading her, filling her.

It had been so long since she'd held a man inside her. So long. And her orgasm never stopped. It eased only slightly before beginning to build again as he moved deeper, drew back, and thrust into her again and again. Her nails raked his back. She whispered words of old, in a tongue long forgotten.

Again the peak burst upon her, and shattered her very being. This time he was there with her, grating his teeth, moan-
ing her name—the name he'd given her. Poppy.

Slowly, their bodies uncoiled. Matthew rolled to the side,
pulling her into his arms, holding her against him. She felt
his heart pounding in his chest. Powerful and strong. Her
own beat rapidly, too. But it wasn't as strong. She could feel,
more than ever, the flaws in its imperfect rhythm. The weakness in its most powerful beat.

He stroked her hair. "What language was it that you were
speaking to me, Poppy?"

She lay against him, loving the feel of strong male arms
around her, no matter what else was wrong in her world.
"Sumerian," she told him. "It was spoken four thousand years
ago, in my homeland."

He nodded. She felt the movement of his head. "Oh, I get
it now. That's where I've heard that name of yours before,
isn't it? You're named for some ancient queen, aren't you?"

She shook her head slowly. "No, Matthew. I'm not named
for anyone."

Rising up on his elbows, he studied her face, a hint of
humor in his eyes. "You mean you actually are some ancient
queen."

"Of course I am."

He bent and kissed her shoulder. "And what were you
saying, my sexy, crazy, Sumerian queen?"

"It was a bit of ancient poetry, part of a song they say the
goddess Inanna sang to her husband. 'Your kiss is like honey.
Touch me and I tremble, my strong, powerful lion. Your kiss
is like honey sweet. Kiss me again.' "

He lifted her chin and kissed her lips, as if in response to
her request. But when he lifted his head away again, his eyes
were serious. "It wasn't a mistake, what just happened, between us."

She shook her head. "No. It can't have been."

He nodded. "I don't want to hurt you the way I've hurt
others in my life, Poppy. Don't let me."

She let her gaze roam his face, his stubbled chin, strong
jaw, full lips. "I'm not the one in danger of getting hurt here."
She lowered her lashes. "Don't get attached to me, Matthew.
I don't have that much more time."

"You've said that before. I'm going to have to insist you tell me what the hell you mean by it this time. Because if you're thinking about—about—"

"Suicide?" she asked. "No. I just . . ." She looked at his face, at the sudden intensity in his eyes, and she couldn't tell him the truth—that she probably wouldn't live very much longer. She knew it, though. Sensed it with every breath she drew. Better to spare him that knowledge. "When we get back to civilization, Matthew, I'm going to leave. You need to know that. Be aware of it. And prepare yourself."

He stared at her. But finally he licked his lips and nodded. "All right. If that's what you have to do, then . . ." Lowering his head, he shook it slowly. "I don't want to think about it, to tell you the truth. Here and now, remember? That's all I want to think about."

She smiled very slightly. "That's good, Matthew. Because here and now is all we have."

He frowned, searching her face, but she said no more. Instead she rolled to her feet, ran into the waves, then dove into the water.

# 8

*Something was wrong with her, he knew it with the same* uncanny clarity with which he knew other things about her. He knew, for example, that she was not an ordinary woman. There was something otherworldly about her. Something older than time. He knew, too, that she hadn't come here by accident. That it had been predestined. That he was supposed to help her in some way. To save her—from what, he wasn't sure. Maybe from whatever it was he sensed was wearing her down.

She wasn't getting stronger here, as he'd expected, but weaker. Day by day, weaker. Sure, she'd recovered somewhat from her ordeal at sea. But this was something else. Something he felt, more than saw. It did show, physically. It showed in how easily she could become breathless. A short walk would do it. It showed in how she grew paler all the time, no matter how much sunlight she got. It showed in her eyes, which revealed pain she wouldn't admit to feeling. But he sensed it even more powerfully. He sensed something in her slowly fading. Like a bright light growing gradually dimmer as its fuel burned away.

They made love, and slept, and woke and made love again, until finally Poppy fell into a deep, heavy sleep. Sensing she wouldn't wake again until morning, he wrapped her in the nearly dry robe, and carried her back to the villa. She never stirred. And maybe it was his imagination, but she seemed lighter than before. Frail and light and cool in his arms. Less substantial than the last time he'd carried her over the same path.

He tucked her into his bed and brushed her hair away from her face. Her skin was cool, and he thought he detected the bare beginnings of shadows beneath her eyes. She was sick. He would lay odds that she'd been sick long before her time in the ocean. She might even be dying.

And she seemed to have accepted it. But she hadn't counted on him. She had no clue as to what the kinds of things a man with his power, his wealth, and his connections, could accomplish. He hadn't been able to save Gabriella. But he would damn well pull out all the stops to save her dark sister.

Her dark sister. When had he begun to think of Poppy that way?

Smiling very slightly, he bent to press a kiss to her forehead. "Don't you worry, Poppy. I'm going to fight this thing. And you're going to fight it with me. I'm not giving you any choice in the matter."

$D$awn broke in neon. Blazing orange and glowing yellow painted her eyelids from beyond the windows and burned through them until she awoke. The light made her head ache, and she immediately turned away from it and groaned.

Then she realized she was in bed. She'd expected to wake up on the beach. In Matthew's arms.

Gods, last night . . . She closed her eyes, remembering. She'd never felt that way before. Not even with Natum. How was that possible? Natum had been the love of her life . . . hadn't he?

She heard voices then and, frowning, got to her feet. Her legs were oddly watery and her head heavy. Still, she moved closer to the door, listening as the voices outside rose.

"It's too soon, I tell you! Why are you so damned stubborn, anyway?"

"I have my reasons, Murial. And since when are you my keeper?"

"Dammit, Matthew, that hurts. I'm your friend. You know that."

His tone was softer when he replied. "I know that. I'm sorry. But I don't want to argue about this anymore. The Weather Service says there's still time. So we're going back—this morning."

There was a long pause. Poppy opened the door a crack and peeked out. She could see down the hall, into the living room where the two stood facing each other. Matthew had a cup of coffee in his hand. Murial looked close to tears.

Backing inside, Poppy gathered her strength and quickly showered and dressed in some of the too-large clothes Matthew had found for her. By the time she joined them, Matthew was putting plates of food on the table and refilling his coffee cup.

He smiled when she came in, pulled out a chair for her. "Morning, Poppy," he said. Gods, if she went by the look in his eyes, she might think he was speaking to someone he cherished. "How are you feeling?"

Odd question, she thought with a frown. "Fine. I'm feeling fine." She slid a glance toward Murial as she sat down. "In fact, I think this island air is good for me. A few more days out here and I'll be as good as new." She forced a bright smile as she spoke the lie.

Matthew set a plate of food in front of her that could have fed three grown men. "I wish I could agree with you, there, but as I've already told Murial, I think we need to get back."

She lifted her gaze to his. "But why? I thought we were going to wait out the storm here."

He shook his head, then took his own seat. "No, that's impossible. For one thing, the Weather Service says the storm is close to hurricane force now. It's moving in, but slowly. They expect it to hit us by nightfall, and it's just not going to be safe here."

She nodded, sliding a surreptitiously apologetic glance at Murial, who was so deep in thought that she didn't even notice. "So it would be too dangerous to stay," she said, looking at Matthew again. "I'm confused, Matthew. Just yesterday, you thought it would be too dangerous to leave."

"We have better information today. There's plenty of time to make the flight back to Miami. We'll be flying away from the storm, and, as I said, it's moving slowly. At this point, it would be far more risky to stay than to go."

Again she nodded. "And what's the other reason?"

"Other reason?" He leaned over to fill her cup with coffee. She hadn't asked. She'd barely glanced at the cup, thought of coffee, and he'd acted. It was as if he could read her thoughts. Or maybe he was just watching her that closely.

"You said, 'for one thing' before you mentioned the storm. That implies some other thing."

He averted his eyes, gave his head a shake. "I'm just ready to go back. I think it's the best thing."

He was keeping something from her. She could barely believe it. She sighed impatiently and ate a few bites of the food, but her stomach didn't receive it well. "You're just going to leave the place to the storm, then?"

"This place isn't that hard to button up," he said, looking relieved at the change of subject. "It's not as if hurricanes are a rarity out here. I'll have the barriers on the windows and doors inside an hour. So finish up your breakfast and grab what you want to take with you." He glanced at his watch. "We'll leave at nine. All right?"

It seemed there was no talking him out of it. And who was she to try, if this was what he felt he needed to do? Maybe it would be good for him to go back, to face his past and deal with his ghosts, despite what Murial thought.

Something twisted into a tight, hard little knot inside her, and she hated to admit that the idea of leaving him, as she knew she would have to do when they arrived back in the States, was painful. Almost unbearable.

*She hadn't arrived on the island with much. Her dagger* and her tattered clothes. So there wasn't much for her to throw into the small bag that Matthew gave her, but she managed to find a few things. The toothbrush and hairbrush he'd given her. The white robe—she'd grown rather attached to the silly oversized thing. And Gabriella's diary. She didn't intend to keep it, of course. But she couldn't bear the thought of leaving it here to be washed away by the storm. She would give it to Matthew before she went on her way to face an uncertain future alone.

Murial climbed into the plane first. She started its engines, and the whir of the propellers sent sea spray flying in a fine mist that dampened anyone who came near. Matthew stood near the front end of the pontoons, untying the rope that held the plane to the island. "Go on, Poppy, climb aboard." He had to shout to make himself heard above the roar of the engines. "I'll have to give this baby a push to get her into the water and turned around."

Nodding, Poppy went to the open door, gripped a handle, and put her foot on a step. She looked up, met Murial's eyes, and returned her ready smile. Then she reached out a hand.

Murial clasped it.

The jolt that rocked through her at that touch would have knocked her down to the sand, if the other woman hadn't held on so tight. Murial tugged, and Puabi found herself pulled right into the plane's cockpit, shoved through a doorway into the rear section, then down into a seat.

She blinked up at Murial, her heart racing. That jolt of contact could only mean one thing. "You . . . you're an Immortal High Witch!"

"A Dark One," she whispered. "Just like you. It took you long enough, Puabi. I was beginning to think you'd never figure it out."

"But . . . but I don't understand. What do you want with Matthew? He's a mortal. He's just an ordinary man."

"Oh, I think we both know there's nothing ordinary about Matthew Fairchild," she said with a slow, wicked smile. "But it isn't him I want. And I'm afraid you aren't going to live long enough to learn any more than that. Neither of you is."

Puabi reached for her dagger, her hand shooting automatically to her thigh. Years of battle had made the reaction a reflex. But her dagger wasn't at her thigh—it was packed in her bag. She'd thought she wouldn't need it at hand at least until they reached the mainland. Gods, when had she become so complacent?

"What's the matter, Puabi? Do you think I want your heart? You know perfectly well that the hearts of the Dark Ones are weak trophies at best, and yours is all but used up. Tell me, Puabi, why haven't you killed one of the Light Ones to rejuvenate yourself? I just can't figure that out."

Puabi surged to her feet, balled up a fist, and swung at
her, but Murial ducked the blow and easily shoved Puabi
down on the seat again. "I don't want to fight you, Puabi. I
just want you out of my way."

She brought her hand around, and Puabi glimpsed the ob-
ject in it. Large, metallic, red. She ducked fast, then drove
her head toward Murial's belly. But the other woman was
faster and stronger—in peak condition, while Puabi was running on empty. Murial simply dodged the attack and swung
again. The small fire extinguisher smashed down on Puabi's
head, and lights exploded in her eyes. Then one by one, they
blinked out. The last thing she heard was Murial's voice,
cruel and deep. "You're going to die, Puabi. For keeps this
time, if you ask me."

*Matthew waded into the surf, tugging the plane easily*
around to face away from the island. Then he used the pontoon as a step, climbed in, and pulled the hatch shut behind
him. "All set," he said, turning to Murial.

She sat at the controls, smiling at him, her light blue eyes
sparkling. "Great. We're on our way. Go on, now, go buckle
up." Even as she spoke, she set the thing in motion. Matthew
turned toward the rear and made his way back, through the
small doorway toward the set of passenger seats, smiling as
he caught sight of Poppy relaxing there. The warmth that
moved through him whenever he saw her was amazing. He
wasn't a fool. He knew damn well that part of the attraction
was her resemblance to Gabriella—the woman he'd taken
for granted and lost. But it wasn't only that. There was something more to Poppy.

Moving nearer, he felt his smile freeze in place and then
slowly change into a frown. "Poppy? Hey, what's wrong?"
She was slumped against one side of the plane, eyes closed,
body limp. He knelt in front of her, gripping her hands,
touching her face. "What is it? Poppy?"

"Anything wrong?" Murial called. "What's going on back
there?" The plane was banging against the incoming waves
now, shuddering a little, but then it lifted off and left the
choppy waters behind.

"It's Poppy. She's out cold." He checked for a pulse, watched her chest, and held his breath until he felt hers whispering from her lips to bathe his face. Finally, he detected the soft thrum of the blood rushing through her veins. "She's alive," he said, as much to confirm it to himself and the universe—to make it so—as to inform Murial. "What the hell happened in here? She seemed fine . . ."

"Damned if I know." The plane was banking now, settling into flight. "She was okay when I helped her aboard. Gee, maybe she's sicker than I realized. I mean, I sensed she wasn't quite well, but I had no idea she was seriously ill."

He sank into the seat beside Poppy, pulling her into a more comfortable position with care. "She is, I'm afraid. That's why I wanted to get back today, Murial. I want her to see the top specialists in the country. The world, if necessary."

"You know what's wrong with her, then?"

"No. I think it may be her heart, but she hasn't told me." He frowned then, as the clouds parted briefly, and the sun slanted through the window. It reflected on something shining or wet in Poppy's hair. Bending closer, he probed with his fingers, and then found the small cut, and felt a knob the size of a goose egg forming around it. "For the love of . . ." He got to his feet and laid her on the seat, then pried back one eyelid with his thumb, trying to check her pupils. "She has a head injury!" he shouted. "Jesus, Murial, something must have happened in here!"

"Oh, no!" Murial said. "You know, I heard her fall, when she was getting into her seat, but she said she was fine. I should have checked."

Matthew grimaced, then went for the first aid kit mounted to the wall nearby. He took out a cold pack and crushed it to activate it, then laid it on Poppy's head. "Hard to believe she could have fallen hard enough to do this much damage," he muttered.

"Look, I'll have you in Miami in under two hours. Just hang in there, okay? She'll be fine."

He nodded. And he sat with Poppy for a time, holding her, speaking softly to her.

It kept getting darker by degrees. It didn't register right away, but when it did, Matthew feared the storm may have

picked up its pace. Maybe it was coming in faster than pre-
dicted. Hell, that was all they needed.

"Better get a weather update," he called to Murial. "I don't
like the looks of this." She didn't answer, and he turned to
shout toward the front. "Murial, did you hear me? I said you
ought to get a storm advisory in case . . ." As he spoke he
glanced out the window, and he was briefly disoriented because the storm clouds were on the wrong side of the plane.
"Jesus, Murial, where the hell are you taking us?"

Still no answer, and his stomach clenched. "Dammit, Murial, answer me!" A rush of air and sound came then. Matthew made his way forward, only to see Murial vanish
through the open hatch. He reached for her but grabbed only
air, and he watched her plummet with a sense of horror before he realized that she was wearing a parachute. It bloomed
far below, and beyond it he saw the familiar shape of Saba.
Then he yanked the hatch closed, his mind racing with questions.

"She's trying to kill us, Matthew. Both of us."

He turned to see Poppy, clinging to the walls to hold herself up, leaning into the cockpit. She looked so weak. "But
I don't understand. Why?"

"There's no time now," she whispered. "Look."

He looked out the windshield, and what he saw made his
heart flip over. The whirling, swirling black sky. Murial had
pointed them directly into the hurricane before bailing.

"Do you know how to fly this thing?" Poppy asked
weakly.

He met her eyes, his own grim. "No."

# 9

*The* engines coughed as if to punctuate his answer, and he scanned the panel to try to figure out why. It wasn't a difficult puzzle. The needle of the fuel gauge pointed to Empty. "She must have dumped the fuel. She wasn't taking any chances." One last sputter, a cough, and the craft began to descend.

"I won't give up without a fight, dammit." Matthew got himself into the seat, took the controls. He'd been in the plane with Murial often enough to have picked up a few things. He found the lever that would lower flaps and, he hoped, slow their airspeed. He used the stick to keep the nose from dipping too low as the plane's engines died all at once. And then they drifted on the air, and he could hear the wind all around them. It was damned eerie.

"Where did she go?" Poppy asked. "How could she jump into all that ocean?"

"Island," he said, his attention on the controls, on the plane, on the water rushing up at them. "Saba. Back there." Faster and faster the sea rose toward him. "Sit down, Poppy! Brace yourself!"

He didn't know if she did or not. They hit, a wing dipped, and the plane cartwheeled. Matthew was tossed around violently as water rushed on him from all directions and his body smashed into hard objects.

And then there was only water. Stillness, and water, all around. He didn't know which way was up or down. So he struggled toward the light. It was all he had to go by.

His head broke the surface. He sucked in a breath, and a wave slapped his face and crawled down his throat. Choking, gasping, and spitting, he tread water, sought air.

Poppy! Jesus, where was she? "Poppy! Poppy, where are you?"

He couldn't see her. God, he couldn't see her! "Poppy!" More water down his throat, in his lungs. Hell, where was she? The sky was black, the wind picking up. A huge wave broke over his head and drove him under. When he tried to struggle to the surface, something bumped his leg.

*Shark.* The word whispered through his mind like a razor-edged blade.

Then the thing bumped him again, its body hitting his. And the next thing he knew he was on the surface, sucking in air.

The animal circled him, arched out of the water, and vanished again. Not a shark. A dolphin.

The clouds burst, and rain fell in a deluge, powerful drops driving into him like icy pellets. He searched for Poppy, screamed her name until he was so hoarse he could barely speak. The waves increased, and he was thrown under again, and again, but each time the dolphin pushed him back up. He was barely conscious the last time it happened, and his hand closed around the dorsal fin.

And suddenly the animal shot forward, cutting through the waves like a knife through butter. He held on for dear life—that was all he could do.

*Matthew coughed, rolled onto his side, choked and* gagged. Water trickled out of his mouth, and he rose up onto all fours, arching his back as his lungs expelled more salt water.

When the spasm ended, he rose to his knees in the black sand, wiping his mouth with the back of his hand. "Poppy," he whispered, staring out to sea. "God, did you make it?"

Something moved in his peripheral vision, and he swung his head around. There, farther along the beach, tangled in seaweed was . . . something. The dolphin?

The tail rose and lowered again. The woman moaned softly. He blinked, and rubbed his eyes. And there was no tail. No mermaid lying there in the sand. There was only Poppy.

He ran forward, fell to his knees beside her, and lifted her slowly. "Baby, Poppy, are you all right?"

Opening her eyes very slowly, she nodded. "I have . . . to tell you . . ."

He pressed a finger to her lips. "No. No, you're too weak. I need to get you to a doctor." He looked around him, frantic. "Wait a minute, this is a black sand beach. And there, there's the crater. See it?"

She looked where he pointed. The peak of the tiny volcano island rose into the storm clouds.

"This is Saba," he told her, scanning the place to get his bearings. "Yes, there's a road off this way. And there's a town a mile farther. God, I hope they haven't evacuated the entire island."

He scooped her up into his arms and carried her. "How did you get to shore, Poppy? God, I was so afraid. I couldn't find you. How did you do it?"

She opened her eyes and stared up at him, her vision unfocused. "I swam. And I pulled you with me."

He frowned, wondering if her fever was back. She'd been through so much. "No, baby. A dolphin towed me in. But it's okay, I understand—"

"It was me. I only made you think I was a dolphin. It was easier than answering all the questions you would have . . ." she turned her head to the side, and coughed.

"But, Poppy, that's impossible."

"No. It's a spell. The *glamourie*. It's only a trick of the mind."

He kept walking, kept carrying her. "Even if you could make me think you were a dolphin, you couldn't swim that fast," he said.

"Yes, I could. Faster, if I were at full strength. But I used up almost every bit of power left in me, Matthew. And I won't last much longer now."

"Yes, you will, dammit. I'll find a doctor. I'll save you, somehow, I swear."

She smiled weakly. "We haven't much time. I must tell you now, what I am. I'm a witch, Matthew. Not an ordinary witch. I am an Immortal High Witch. I've been alive for more than four thousand years. I survive by taking the lives of others like me. Taking their hearts—"

"No."

"Yes, it's true. Just listen to me, I beg of you!"

He swallowed hard, tried to walk faster. The village he sought was in sight now. The road was muddy and slick, the rain coming down in sheets. "If you're immortal, then you can't die. Yet you keep telling me you're not going to live much longer."

"We die. And we revive again. Over and over, but only so long as our stolen power holds out. At least that's how it is for the Dark Ones, like me. I could make myself strong again by killing another. But . . . something has changed, Matthew. I can't do it anymore."

He closed his eyes briefly. It was insanity, she was talking insanity!

"Murial is what I am. She's the same. And she wants something from you. I don't know what. I cannot even guess, but there's something. You have to kill her, Matthew. You have to kill her, and there are very few ways you can do that."

His jaw was clenched, rain streaming down his face. Her hair was plastered to her head, her clothes to her body.

"You need to cut out her heart. And when that's done, you must burn her body, and her heart as well. That will release her spirit. And Matthew . . . you must do the same to me."

"This is ridiculous! You're talking crazy. You aren't going to die, Poppy, you—"

"Please," she whispered. "Promise me you'll see to it that my wishes are carried out."

He stared down at her as he trudged onward, through the rain. "All right. If . . . if the worst should happen, I'll see to it."

She nodded slowly, relaxing in his arms, and he figured it was worth it, making that ridiculous promise, if it eased her mind. He'd be damned before he would do it, though.

"You were right, you know," she murmured. "I did wash up on your island for a reason. I think it was to save you from drowning, and now that I've done that, I probably won't live much longer. It doesn't seem like enough—to redeem me, I mean. But it's something, anyway."

She closed her eyes then.

Matthew stopped walking. Her head tipped back and hung limply. He shook her. "Poppy? Poppy, dammit, don't you go! Not yet, not like this. I love you, do you hear me? I don't give a shit what you did in the past, or what kind of monster you think you are. I love you. Dammit, Poppy, I love you!"

No response. He looked up, and saw a miracle standing in front of him, in the form of a sign carved in wood, with an arrow pointing to the right. The sign read, SABA MEDICAL CLINIC.

# 10

The clinic was in a large house in the middle of a banana plantation, and he guessed the doctor who ran it likely lived in it as well. He hoped desperately that someone was home, as he carried Poppy to the door and pounded on it.

A light came on within. Footsteps. Then a tall, almost regal-looking dark-skinned woman opened it. She wore white, and her name tag called her Aliyah. "Please," he said. "She needs help."

"Of course! Come in! What's happened to her?" She barely glanced at Poppy as she led them quickly into a room and pointed to a bed. "There, lay her down there. I'll call Dr. Sloane."

Matthew laid Poppy in the bed, noticing that she wasn't the only patient. There was another bed in the room, a curtain drawn around it, in typical hospital-room fashion, to block it from view, but he could hear the steady beep of some kind of monitor. The nurse had depressed a button on the wall and was now leaning over Poppy, one hand to her cheek.

But then she sucked in a breath and jerked backward, her eyes widening. "I don't . . . I don't understand . . ."

Poppy drew a shuddering breath and opened her eyes. "I'm so cold," she whispered.

Shaking herself, the nurse pointed at the closet. "There are dry nightgowns in there. And blankets. Get them. Go!"

He did, and by the time he came back with the requested items, she had efficiently stripped Poppy of her soaking-wet clothes and dried her with towels. She dressed her quickly in a white flannel nightgown, then had Matthew lift her up so she could strip away the wet bedding and briskly put warm, dry sheets on the bed. Then he laid her down again and tucked blankets around her.

The nurse stuck a thermometer into her mouth and was taking Poppy's pulse when the sound of shuffling steps alerted him, and he turned to see an aging man with skin so tanned it stood in shocking contrast to his snow-white hair. He was in his seventies, easily. "Well, now, what have we here? A couple of refugees from the storm? Should have evacuated with the others, son."

"We were in a small plane that veered off course and went down," Matthew explained. "We were lucky to make it to the shore."

The old man arched his brows in surprise. "My God, you're lucky to be alive!" He nodded to the nurse. "Go on and find this fellow some dry clothes. I'll see to the girl."

"A moment, please, Dr. Sloane?"

He glanced up at the nurse, who stood beside Poppy's bed, leaning over her. She sent him a look filled with meaning, and he frowned and went closer. Aliyah nodded at Poppy, and the old man looked down. Then he blinked, and his brows drew close. "How in the . . ."

"Why do you both keep looking at me so strangely?" Poppy asked, a hint of her former haughty attitude making its way into her tone. It did Matthew a world of good to hear it.

"I . . . well, I . . . you look very much like . . . someone."

"Yes, she does," Matthew said, coming closer. "She looks like my late wife, Gabriella."

"Gabriella," the nurse whispered, and she crossed herself. "Jesus, Joseph, and Mary."

"What the hell is the matter with the two of you?" Matthew demanded.

"Go on, Aliyah," the doctor said. "Get those dry things for the young man." She left, and the doctor seemed to square his frail shoulders as he faced Matthew. "I'm Alan Sloane," he said.

"Matthew. Matthew Fairchild. Now, can we skip the part where we discuss the weather and get to the point here? I can see something isn't right."

Dr. Sloane nodded slowly. "You're quite right about that. You see, about three months ago a patient—a young woman who looked remarkably like this one," he said with a nod at Puabi, "was transferred here to this clinic. Brain-dead, but on full life support. Her sister paid us a generous amount— enough to keep the clinic running for years—to keep her here, and care for her until—"

Matthew turned slowly, his eyes moving from the doctor's to that closed curtain that surrounded the other bed. Another patient. She looked like Poppy. And she'd been here for three months. His knees jelled, and Poppy reached out from her bed to clasp his hand.

More clearly than before, now, he heard the steady beeps and the pumping and hissing of the machines that kept some-one alive according to some warped definition of the word. He pulled free of Poppy's hand and walked toward the cur-tains.

"There's more," the doctor began.

But he tugged the white curtains open. There, in the bed, lay Gabriella, her skin pale and waxy. Her hair neat and short. They'd cut it, probably to make it easier to care for her. It was as short as Poppy's now. But the biggest differ-ence in his young wife, was the swollen mound that was her belly, expanded to the size of a beach ball underneath the sheets. And even as he stared at it in utter shock and total disbelief, the child inside her moved. He saw it.

"Sweet Jesus," Matthew whispered as he dropped to his knees, unable to hold his emotions in check any longer.

*Puabi* ignored the sudden skipping of her heart, like a motor working to keep from stalling. She couldn't focus on herself now. Not with Matthew on his knees, his entire body shaking with the force of his emotions. She glanced at the doctor. "Give us just a moment, will you?"

"No, not yet. You need medical attention, and I need answers." He moved toward Matthew, clasped his shoulder from behind. "As no doubt, you do as well. Is this woman your wife?"

"Yes." The word was stark, and Puabi felt the pain in it. She struggled to sit up in the bed.

"And what happened to her, so far as you knew, I mean?"

Swallowing hard, Matthew lifted his head, but his eyes never left the body of that small woman in the bed. Puabi understood that, because she couldn't take her eyes off the woman either. So like her. And yet, softer somehow. And the fact that her belly was swollen with a child she would never know seemed like a twist of fate too cruel to bear. Why? "She could be my sister," Puabi heard herself whisper. "My small, frail little sister . . ."

"She was in a car accident. Her body—someone's body—was burned beyond recognition. We . . . we thought she was dead. I buried her, I—God, Gabriella . . ."

"And her sister? The one who brought her here to us, made these arrangements for us to keep her on life support until the baby was born—she never told you?"

He finally looked away from his wife, his head turning slowly to face the doctor. "She doesn't have a sister."

"Murial," Puabi whispered. "It had to be Murial." Her heart shuddered, and she tried to catch her breath without letting on that she was in distress. Short, shallow, open-mouthed breaths were all she could manage. She got to her feet, somehow, moved until she was at Gabriella's bedside. And once there, she reached out and touched the face of the woman in the bed, the woman who looked so very much like her.

"You really could be my little sister."

Matthew lifted his gaze to the doctor's. "The baby? It's . . . all right?"

Puabi glanced downward at the swollen belly and lowered her hand gently to it. She could feel the life force inside, powerful and strong. "Fine. The baby's fine," she said, a little louder now, a smile pulling at her lips.

Dr. Sloane clasped Matthew's hand and helped him to his feet as they both looked at Puabi. The doctor seemed puzzled, but he nodded. "Yes, you're right. The baby appears to be perfectly healthy in every way. In fact, we'd originally scheduled the C-section for tomorrow. Though we may very well have to put it off another day if this storm hits the way they're predicting it will."

Matthew's eyes turned bleak. "What about that, Dr. Sloane? The storm, I mean. If the power goes out—"

"We're prepared for that. We have a backup generator. It kicks on automatically, son. The baby will be safe until its birth, we'll see to that."

Matthew nodded, seeming relieved, but only for a moment. Then he looked grim again. "And then what?" he asked.

Puabi returned her hand to the woman's face and stroked her hair, feeling an odd ripple of emotion that she had never felt before. *Never.*

Dr. Sloane looked at Gabriella, his expression sad. "She's not going to come out of the coma. She's brain-dead, son, she has been for months. The kind thing to do, the only decent thing to do, would be to take her off the life support. Let her go."

As had happened before, Puabi's heart seemed to skip, leaving her short of breath. Then it contracted—as if being slowly squeezed by a large, powerful hand.

The steady, monotonous pattern of the beeps emanating from the machine behind her suddenly changed. Rapid-fire, then slowing.

Matthew looked up sharply, and Dr. Sloane literally lunged toward the bed. Puabi stepped away to give him room as he put his stethoscope into his ears and pressed it to Gabriella's chest.

"What was that, Doctor? What happened?" Matthew asked.

The doctor held up a hand, frowning, listening. He shook his head. "Her heartbeat is fine. Must have been a glitch in the monitor." But he still looked puzzled.

Puabi was too dizzy by now to stand up without giving herself away, so she sat down in a chair in the corner. The nurse had gone to get those dry clothes the doctor had requested for Matthew. And the two men seemed too busy fussing over Gabriella to notice her.

The nurse returned, her arms full of clothes for Matthew. She handed them over, then frowned at Poppy. "You ought to be in bed. We haven't even examined you yet."

"I'm fine," she said. "Really, I'm feeling much better." She couldn't lie down. Not yet. She was too tired, and she was afraid—so afraid—that if she rested, she might slip away. She might die, for the final time. And now—now she sensed that her mission, her reason for washing up into Matthew's life—was not yet complete. There was more. It had to do with Gabriella. And her child.

Dr. Sloane said, "I'll leave you alone for a minute or two now. But not long. I want to examine you, young lady." He nodded to Matthew. "I'll be nearby. Call if you need me."

Matthew nodded, never opening his eyes until the doctor left them and closed the door. Then, he went to Poppy in the chair, knelt in front of her, clasped her hands. "Are you all right?"

She smiled through moist eyes. "Me? Matthew, how can you think of me when you're going through so much?"

"Because I care about you, as much as you detest hearing sappy emotional garbage like that. And I can see you're feeling like hell right now. And because I know what a shock all of this is to you, walking in here, seeing her for the first time. The baby . . ." He looked toward the bed.

"It's a boy, you know," she whispered. "A son, like the son I carried, and bore. Only yours is strong and healthy."

He sighed deeply, shaking his head. "Why is fate so damned cruel, Poppy? Why did a healthy, loving mother like you have to lose her child? Why does a strong, healthy baby have to lose his mother?"

She shook her head slowly. "I don't know. I only know that you need to grab on to whatever joy you find in life. And you've just found some, Matthew. You have a son on the way. You won't be left alone. You'll be a father. That's what you need to focus on here. Not losing Gabriella. Not even losing me. But the joy of this gift. This miracle." Her eyes seemed too heavy to keep open. She was so tired all of a sudden.

She expected him to look toward the woman in the bed again, as she did, but instead he frowned. "Poppy?" His palm pressed to her cheek. "Poppy, what is it? Dammit, you're in trouble, aren't you? Poppy?"

But she only smiled weakly at him and slipped into sleep as Matthew shouted for the doctor.

*There* was *chaos. Dr. Sloane, Matthew, and Aliyah* surrounded Poppy's hospital bed.

"I called for more help, Doctor," Aliyah said. "They're on the way."

"We're losing her," the doctor yelled.

Aliyah raced into the hall, and when she came back three other strangers followed, two women and a young man. Aliyah pushed a large box with ominous paddles attached.

"Oh, God, no . . . no, please." Matthew's heart was breaking. Jesus, this couldn't be happening.

"What the . . . what the *hell?*" The nurse beside him exclaimed.

He glanced at her, saw her gaze riveted on Gabriella's monitor. And when he followed that gaze, he saw erratic spikes and valleys in the lines on the screen, heard its frenzied beeping, totally out of rhythm.

"Doctor!" the nurse shouted as she rushed to Gabriella's side.

"Not now," the doctor yelled. Then he shouted, "Clear!" and Matthew saw Poppy's body arch off the bed.

"No good," someone said. "Hit her again."

"For the love of God, Dr. Sloane!" the nurse near Gabriella said.

The doctor looked up, started to say something, then stopped as his eyes raked over Gabriella's monitor. Frowning, he handed the paddles over to a nearby set of hands. "Keep working on her, Sally. I'll only be a sec."

Sally took the paddles. "Let's try again," she said. She nodded to the woman who was slowly squeezing air into Poppy's lungs, even as Dr. Sloane crossed the room to Gabriella.

"Clear!" Sally yelled.

This time, Matthew was looking at Gabriella. And he saw *her* body arch off the bed in response to the electric shock jolting through *Poppy's* heart.

Dr. Sloane froze in his tracks and crossed himself.

Sally said, "Wait a minute, wait a minute—"

"We have sinus rhythm, Doctor," a nurse said from near Poppy's side. "She's back."

Dr. Sloane turned to Gabriella's monitor, and Matthew saw it was again bleeping in normal time, with regular patterns in the lines on the screen. "My God, I've never . . . my God!" Sloane looked from one monitor to the other.

So did everyone else.

What they saw, Matthew realized, was two women who looked damn near identical to one another, and two hearts beating out an identical pattern. The beeping of the machines sounded like one louder beep. The patterns on the monitors were a perfect match.

Dr. Sloane said to a nurse, "I want printouts of both EKGs over the past"—he glanced at his watch—"ten minutes." Then he turned to Matthew. "You said Gabriella didn't have a sister. Are you sure? Could these two be sisters—twins?"

"I don't know."

"Hell, even if they were, it wouldn't explain . . ." He looked at the nurse who had first alerted him to Gabriella's condition. The one he'd called Sally.

"Yes, Dr. Sloane," she said. "I saw it, too."

"So did I," Aliyah said.

Dr. Sloane shook his head slowly. "Let's just see to it that they stay stable until we can figure this out." He looked at Matthew. "Son, do you know anything at all about your . . . Poppy, you call her?"

"Her name is Puabi. Poppy's . . . just a nickname."

"Do you know anything about her medical condition?"

He shook his head. "I think she believes she's dying. That her heart is wearing out and that nothing can be done."

"Do you know where she's from? A family doctor? Anything?"

"No. No, I'm sorry. She came here from Maine, but that's not where she's from. She . . . told me once that she was born in the desert. I think it's Iraq nowadays, but . . ." He stopped, unsure of whether to continue. She'd also said she was four thousand years old, an ancient queen, a witch, and some kind of shape-shifter. Was he supposed to tell the old doc all of that, too?

Frowning, Dr. Sloane squeezed his shoulder.

"The baby's still fine," Sally announced, removing her

stethoscope and smoothing the blankets gently back over Gabriella.

"Thank goodness," Aliyah said, as she ever so carefully taped Poppy's IV in place, her eyes tender and caring.

"Good. That's something to cling to, then, isn't it?" Sloane said. "I've got tests to run. Calls to make while we still have phone lines. We may need more expertise than I have to figure this out, young man, but I promise you, I'm going to give it my best shot. For now . . . well, you need to get into those dry clothes. Get warm, and get some rest."

"I'm not leaving them."

Sloane sighed. "I figured you'd say something like that. Stay in here, then, but the rest still goes. I'm going to have nurses watching them both round the clock. Once we get through this damned storm, we'll bring in cardiologists to examine . . . Puabi. Okay?"

Matthew looked at Poppy in the bed, nodded slowly. "Okay."

Dr. Sloane turned to leave. Then he turned back. "Puabi. Wasn't that the name of some ancient queen of . . . Babylon or something?"

"Sumer," Matthew said vaguely. "Four thousand years ago."

"Right. Sumer." He clapped Matthew on the shoulder. "Let's just get them through the storm, okay? Let's just focus on that, and we'll move on from there. All right, Matthew?"

Matthew nodded. But somehow he didn't think there was going to be an aftermath to the storm that approached outside. He felt certain it would sweep down and swallow up his entire world.

# 11

*Hours later, Matthew sat in a chair against the rear* wall, with his dead—or was she only partly dead?—wife on his right side and the woman he loved on his left. His child's life seemed to hang in the balance. No matter how often Dr. Sloane assured him that his son would be fine whatever else might happen, Matthew found himself doubting it. How could anything be fine? The two women he'd cared for more than anything else in his life were dying, as if in some twisted brand of cosmic synchronicity. God, it was as if the two were connected somehow, the way their hearts seemed to beat almost as one.

No. Not almost. Not almost at all. He was freaking trapped in some esoteric *Twilight Zone* episode, with no script and no control. Jesus, it was maddening!

Outside, the storm unleashed its full might on the tiny island. It raged. It clawed at the windows and pounded on the walls as if determined to get inside. It didn't take much imagination to think of the storm as some dark-robed angel of death, storming the gates—on its way here to collect a soul or two.

Or three?

"You're not taking them," Matthew whispered. "I'm not gonna let you take them, dammit."

But the storm raged even harder. Something smashed against the windows—a limb, or perhaps a sign ripped from some nearby business. The safety glass shattered but didn't break apart. A corner of something wooden stabbed through, then the wind tore it free, and the rain and wind sluiced in through the hole. Matthew was on his feet instantly, even as one of the nurses rushed in to help. He balled up a spare blanket from the foot of Poppy's bed and crammed it into the hole. The wind stopped rushing in. The rain was blocked out. He lowered his head in a bone-deep sigh of relief . . .

. . . and then the lights went out. The steady beats of the heart monitors stopped, and their screens went dark. The machine that had been pumping air into Gabriella's lungs stopped its hissing.

"Gabriella! God, the baby!"

Immediately, even before Matthew finished shouting in alarm, the lights came back on, as the backup generator kicked in. So did the monitors. But their tones were long and steady, and the lines on their screens, flat.

The life-support machine did not come back on. The nurse, Aliyah, started hitting its buttons, her eyes growing more and more desperate as she tried to make the machine work. Then suddenly the control panel popped and sent a shower of sparks out from it like a fireworks display. Aliyah backed away, shielding her face with her arms.

"Dammit, do something!" Matthew cried. He turned to Poppy, fell to his knees beside the bed, and gripped her cool hand. Her monitor was flat-lined as well, he realized in horror, droning its steady death tone. "Don't go! For the love of God, don't do this, Poppy, please . . ."

"Start CPR!" Sloane shouted. Sally, one other nurse, and a young man crowded around Poppy and followed his instructions. Pumping her chest. Forcing air into her lungs by squeezing a bag. The doctor turned back to Aliyah, who was doing likewise to Gabriella. "Keep her oxygenated or we'll lose the baby!" he shouted toward the door. "Get a surgical tray in here!"

Matthew didn't know whom he was shouting to. The old guy must have rounded up a few more volunteers, or he'd had others here that Matthew hadn't yet encountered. Within seconds an older, white-haired woman was wheeling a tray into the room. She might even have been Mrs. Sloane.

"What the hell is wrong with the machine?" Matthew demanded, still clinging to Poppy's hand, his own tears streaming freely now as he watched Aliyah and Dr. Sloane working frantically on Gabriella. "Why isn't it working?"

The older woman bared Gabriella's belly and was swabbing it with horrible-looking reddish-brown disinfectant. The others still worked over Poppy, stopping every few seconds to try to find a pulse—only to go right back to pumping her chest again.

"Try to stay calm, Matthew," Dr. Sloane said, his voice loud to overcome the noise in the room and the storm raging outside. "We have to take the baby now, and a C-section is a remarkably fast procedure." Sloane looked across the room. "How's Poppy doing?"

They paused in working on her and checked again. "We have a heartbeat, Doctor," Sally reported, with a sigh of relief. "Weak but steady."

"Thank God," Matthew muttered, his head falling forward, his neck like water.

The curtain around Gabriella was pulled shut, and Matthew had no choice but to let them be. Let them work to save his child. He focused his attention on Poppy, sitting close to her, right on the edge of her bed, holding her hand, stroking her hair. "If you can just get through the storm, Poppy. Things will be better then. We're going to find you the best specialists there are. You're going to be . . ."

"We're losing the fetal heartbeat, Doctor!"

The voice from beyond the curtain made Matthew's own heart stand still. Then suddenly Poppy's hand tightened on his. He looked at her, saw her eyes open and clear. She smiled gently at him. "Don't worry about the baby, Matthew. I'm not finished yet."

"God, Poppy," he whispered. "Honey, it's all right. You're going to be all right."

She shook her head slowly. "I'm done, either way. What power I have left . . ." She stopped talking and stared past him, her gaze turning more intense than he'd yet seen it. He followed her gaze and saw the slight gap in the curtains, and Gabriella's lifeless face visible there.

"Scalpel," the doctor said from beyond the curtain. "Hurry, dammit!"

"The baby's back," Aliyah said. She sighed and even laughed slightly. "Must have been a glitch in the monitor."

Poppy's hand on Matthew's went slack. He turned back to her. Her eyes were still open. But she was gone. He knew it in that single glance. The life was gone, the light in her eyes extinguished. Matthew heard her heart monitor's tone turn to a steady drone once more. "No," he cried. "Oh, Poppy, no."

"Keep the oxygen coming," the doctor said. "Stop CPR so I can make the incision."

"Doctor . . . wait. Don't make that cut!" Aliyah said.

"Why the hell not, Nurse?"

"I . . . I'm getting a pulse."

Minutes ticked by, and the storm raged.

Sally and the others at Poppy's bedside worked on her as before, pumping her chest, but it was different this time. Matthew was holding her hand, and he felt the truth with gut-wrenching clarity. This wasn't Poppy anymore. It was as if she'd pulled her tender hand away and left him holding an empty glove. It was just like that. She was gone. God in heaven, she was gone.

Kneeling on the floor beside the bed, he tipped his head skyward. "Why? For the love of God, will somebody please tell me why? Poppy, Poppy . . ." He lowered his head, sobbing now, unashamed. He loved her. And she was gone.

Behind him, the nurse put her hand on his shoulder, and he heard her breath hitch in her throat, as the others who were crowded around Poppy seemed to realize the futility of their desperate attempts to revive her. "I'm so sorry," someone said.

Brushing the tears from his cheeks, he managed to pull himself to his feet again. Leaning over Poppy, he kissed her gently, and then with hands that trembled he closed her lapis-blue eyes.

His stomach in knots, he turned, wondering if he would come away from this night with anything but loss and heartache. His entire body ached with the loss of the only woman he'd ever loved. He parted the curtain, and no one tried to stop him. He looked at Gabriella on the table. At the others standing around her, just staring at her, and at the heart monitor, which was beeping, showing spiked lines instead of a flat one, even though no one was doing CPR, and the life-support system was a smoking, burned-out wreck.

"What's . . . going on?" he asked, unable to speak above a whisper. And then, suddenly, Gabriella opened her mouth and sucked in a harsh, desperately sharp breath, as her body arched itself off the bed.

Then she relaxed again, falling against the pillows.

"Normal sinus rhythm, Doctor." Aliyah said the words, but they were a bare whisper, and her eyes registered sheer disbelief.

"My God," Sloane said, "she's breathing on her own." He turned to the others. "She's *breathing on her own.*"

Matthew stared at Gabriella's face, rubbed his eyes, and stared some more. He didn't understand what was happening.

"The heartbeat is getting stronger, Doctor," another nurse said.

Sloane said, "I can't believe this."

Then the impossible happened. Gabriella opened her eyes.

But they were not Gabriella's eyes. They were not ebony. They were a startlingly bright blue, flecked with gold, like lapis stones. "Matthew?" she whispered, and her voice was harsh with disuse.

There was stunned silence in the room. Then a burst of activity as they all bent toward her, whipping out penlights and stethoscopes. Matthew shoved them all away. "Please, please, just . . . just for a second."

They backed away mere inches, Dr. Sloane never taking his eyes off the monitors. Matthew bent toward her, frowning as he searched her face, not seeing Gabriella—seeing Poppy instead. He didn't know how, he didn't know why, he didn't even believe it fully. He glanced toward the bed on the other side of the room, but he could make no sense of it.

He turned back to the woman in the bed, fixed his gaze on her eyes once again. "Tell me your name," he whispered.

She frowned at him. "You know my name. It's Puabi. Even if you do refuse to use it." And her smile was weak. "To be honest, I like when you call me Poppy." Her gaze slid lower, then suddenly widened when she saw the shape of her belly under the blankets. "What—Matthew, what's happening? Why am I . . . where is . . . ?"

She lifted her head from the pillows, glancing across the room to the body in the other bed. "Gabriella?" she whispered. Then she looked up at Matthew again, her eyes round and confused. "Why did we change beds?" she asked. Then she frowned. "Why did we change *clothes*?"

Then slowly, her brows lifted and she met Matthew's eyes. "Oh, by the Gods, Matthew . . . I think I'm in Gabriella's . . ." But she didn't finish the sentence. Instead she grimaced and grabbed her belly.

"What is it? What's wrong?"

Poppy looked back at him. No doubt about it. It was Poppy, not Gabriella. And she said, "I think I'm in labor."

*The labor hit hard and fast, and Puabi was already* dizzy with confusion. It was as if she were trapped in some kind of dream where everything she had known was changed. Altered. Her senses seemed dulled, as if she were seeing and hearing everything through a filter. Gone were the sharply honed senses of four thousand years of living as an immortal. Gone.

And her heart . . . it beat in her chest powerfully. She'd become adept over the centuries at feeling her heart, knowing its condition. Moments ago, she'd known it was weak, winding down like an old clock, and probably beating its last. She'd known she had very little power or magick left in her, and she had willed every ounce of it to Gabriella's unborn child. Whatever strength she had, she'd consciously sent to him, realizing at last that saving Matthew's son was the mission she'd been meant to accomplish. And that it would be her last deed on Earth.

Now, though, she felt a strong, steady beat in her chest. A healthy heart.

A healthy *mortal* heart.

And with it, an iron manacle of pain, tightening around her belly and lower back. She gritted her teeth and came upright in the bed, and Matthew held her hand and stared at her in shock and wonder. Gods, he must be as confused as she was by all this!

The doctor and his nurses swarmed, and argued. She was too weak for a natural birth. It was too risky. She was too weak for surgery, it could kill her. And the contractions came hard and fast, and one of the nurses nurse said, "Doctor, this baby is coming. Now!"

Matthew leaned closer, his hand fisted around hers, his face close to hers. He couldn't seem to take his eyes off her, kept checking and rechecking to be sure she was who she was. Hell, *she* wasn't even sure who she was anymore. He stroked her hair, bathed her face with cool water. Talked to her as she struggled to give birth, while the storm outside raged on and on. And mingled with the pain were memories, images, and sounds floating through her mind of a past that was not her own. She remembered the day she had told Matthew she was pregnant. She remembered the day they'd been married.

How could that be? She wasn't Gabriella!

Then she was pushing, and all her attention was focused on the task. Nothing else dared distract her.

Finally, what seemed like hours later, she felt the pressure ease in a rush. She fell backward onto the pillows, her hair damp with sweat, her new heart pounding fiercely in her chest, breath rushing in and out of her lungs.

And then a sound, soft and congested, rose up like the most fragile bleat of a newborn lamb. A sound she had longed to hear for longer than any woman ever had. Her newborn child's first cry.

Puabi blinked and met Matthew's eyes. They were wet and locked on hers. And he tore them away only when Aliyah came between them to lower the baby, wet and slick and wrapped in a tiny blanket, into her arms. The nurse said, "I've seen a lot of things. But tonight, I've witnessed my first honest-to-goodness miracle." She smiled, tears rolling down both cheeks. "Welcome back, Gabriella."

Puabi frowned at the name. "But I'm not . . ." she began, but Matthew shook his head at her. She licked her lips. "Thank you."

The nurse backed away, and Matthew leaned close to her, bent to kiss her forehead, and then the baby's. "Our son," he said.

"Our . . . but . . . ohhh," she whispered, losing track of her

confusion when she looked at the tiny face, the wrinkled little
nose and hazy blue eyes. "Oh, how can this be real?" she
whispered. "How can this be real?" Her own tears flooded,
and though she tried to contain them, they overpowered her.
Her entire body shook with the force of the emotional storm
raging inside her every bit as powerfully as the one outside.
Sobs bent her over her child, and her tears rained down on
his beautiful face.

Aliyah reappeared, easing the baby from her arms. "It's
overwhelming, I know. It's all right, honey. We'll take the
baby just for a few minutes. The doctor needs to be sure he's
a hundred percent. I'll bring him back all clean and dry for
you soon. You rest with your husband now. You two have
so much to talk about."

Puabi nodded, still sobbing, and Matthew put his arms
around her, pulled her close to him, and just held her while
she cried.

# 12

*Everyone left the room, though she doubted they had left* the clinic, since the storm still threw its temper tantrum outside.

"Matthew," a voice said from the doorway. "My God, I can't believe you survived it."

Poppy looked up and saw her. Murial, standing there, wet from the rain, and vicious. "I see your girlfriend wasn't so lucky," she added with a nod toward the body on the other side of the room. The body that had housed Puabi.

"Think again, Murial," Poppy said. She pushed back the covers, darting a quick glance around the room and seeing the stainless-steel surgical tray, which had been pushed aside but not yet removed.

Murial frowned at her. "Gabriella? But you were braindead."

"You made sure of that, didn't you!"

Matthew rose, standing between Poppy and Murial. "What do you mean by that?"

"Oh, it was no accident that night, Matthew. And it wasn't a suicide attempt, either. This bitch ran me off the road. She pulled me out of the wreckage and bashed my head in with a tire iron. She had a life-support unit in the back of a van, ready and waiting. This was all planned."

"Honey," he whispered. He was facing Murial but darting odd, worried glances at her. "How can you know this?"

"I don't know. But I do. I remember it very clearly. Just as clearly as I remember my days on the throne of Sumer and my time on that island with you." She fought the confusion and went on, letting the words come as they would. "She tossed some other body into the car, torched it, and brought me here, claiming to be my sister. She asked them to keep my body functioning until I could deliver the baby—and then to pull the plug."

"Very good," Murial murmured, stepping forward. Matthew moved toward her, but Poppy got to her feet and stepped around him.

"This is my fight, my love."

"You're weak," he said.

Murial smiled. "Not to mention mortal. Don't bother sacrificing yourself, Gabriella." Then she frowned and looked more closely. "Or is it Puabi?"

"I have a feeling it's both," Poppy replied. "And we'd both die happily before we'd let you touch our child."

Murial looked confused, but only briefly. She kept glancing toward the other bed, with the sheet-draped body, then back at Poppy again.

"What do you want with my son, Murial?" Matthew asked. "What the hell can you possibly want with him?"

She lifted her brows. "I'm sure by now you know what I am," she said. And when he nodded, she continued. "Every witch has a certain gift. It's enhanced to incredible degrees in Immortal ones. Hers used to be the *glamourie*," she said, with a nod toward the bed. "Oh, yes, she could make you see her any way she wished. Mine was the gift of prophecy. I see into the future. Not everything, but certain things. I knew your son would be born with a very special power—one I want to make my own. And there's only one way to do that."

"Over my dead body," Poppy said, and she reached out and snatched the scalpel from the tray. She lunged past Matthew as Murial crouched and whipped out her own dagger.

Footsteps came from the hallway. Poppy saw Aliyah step into view, the baby in her arms.

Murial laughed aloud, the sound long and low and evil.

"Ahh, my delivery is here." She clutched the dagger in her fist, lifting it high, and turned toward the baby.

Poppy screamed and launched herself, even as Matthew did the same.

But at that very instant a horrendous crack and a terrible roar split the air. The entire ceiling came down on them all, leaving a cloud of dust and water. Rain flooded in, and the wind whipped, roared, tore through the place. Curtains flew, objects went sailing around the room, crashing into walls.

She pushed the debris off her. She hurt everywhere, but nothing seemed broken. She got to her feet. Matthew was beside her, his arms around her. And Murial? Poppy glimpsed one pale, bloody hand, sticking out from beneath a massive beam.

She didn't even spare the woman a moment's attention as she climbed over the rubble in search of her child.

Aliyah was still standing, several feet away. She'd turned her back to the storm and was hunched over the baby protectively, and the others were even now rushing to her. Matthew took his son gently and held him very close. He held Poppy to his side with his other arm. "We need to get out of here."

Dr. Sloane gestured them toward the exit. "My truck is right out front. We can make it into town, to the shelter. It'll be safe there."

Matthew nodded, and they all started toward the front door.

Poppy stopped herself. Then she turned back toward the rubble, beneath which Murial lay. "Go on, take the baby," she shouted above the wind and rain. "I need to finish this."

"I'm not going anywhere without you, Poppy. Your son needs you now."

"But—"

"You're finished with that, Poppy. That part of your life is over. Now, come on."

She blinked, and swallowed hard. Could it be true? Would she never have to kill another being again? Never have to carve out a heart to ensure her own survival? Was it even possible?

She didn't have time to find out. More of the roof came down, and Murial was buried under so much rubble that

Puabi realized heavy equipment would be needed to dig her out. The house shuddered under the force of the storm, and Matthew pulled her outside. He held her tightly as they raced for the doctor's SUV. Then they all crowded into it, and Dr. Sloane drove them over the muddy, rutted roads and through the fury of the storm toward town.

*D*awn broke, and Poppy stood in the warm sunshine and the slight tropical breeze, surveying the rubble that had been the Saba Medical Clinic. She held her son in her arms, and Matthew stood beside her.

She'd slept like a rock last night, her husband and child snuggled close. But so far she hadn't so much as changed the darling baby's diaper. Too many willing volunteers at the shelter were loathe to see her lift a finger after her ordeal. She had become a local celebrity—the comatose woman who had given birth during a storm and somehow returned to life.

"She's gone," Poppy said softly, staring at the collapsed house, knowing that Murial was no longer trapped beneath the rubble.

"How can you be so sure?"

"I don't know. I feel it."

"I thought you weren't a witch anymore, Poppy."

She smiled up at him. "I'm not an immortal anymore. There's a difference."

He led her to a large rock and helped her to sit down on it. Soon the boat he had sent for would be arriving to carry them back to Miami, and Poppy would begin her new life— as a mortal woman, wife, and mother. It would be odd. And yet, she thought, it was a dream come true.

"Why did she want the baby?" Matthew asked. "I just can't understand why she would think he would have any kind of . . . power she might be able to steal."

"I don't know. I don't understand it." The baby whimpered, and Poppy unfastened the front of the borrowed blouse she wore, held him to her breast, and watched him suckle with a sense of wondrous ecstasy enveloping her entire body.

Close by her side, Matthew stroked her hair and watched his child take nourishment. "Poppy, what do you think happened here last night?"

She sighed deeply. "It goes back a lot further than last night," she whispered. "Matthew, when I lost my first child, I think a part of me died with him. The good part. I went mad. I turned into . . . something else. Something dark, without any light at all in me. It was something I was never meant to be. By using the foulest black magic, the darkest of the dark arts, I kept myself alive. For four thousand years I lived on, at the expense of the lives of others. But in all that time, part of me was gone. Part of me, the good part, had moved on without me."

She ran her fingertips over the baby's face. Gods, but it was so soft.

"It was Gabriella," he said softly. "It was her, wasn't it?"

"I think so. I think she was the part of me that moved on. You said yourself that she never seemed whole. That she craved something she couldn't seem to identify, much less obtain. And that resonated so well with me, because I'd always felt the same. She was lightness without dark. I was darkness without light. I think we were reunited last night—somehow, we melded."

He nodded, staring into her eyes. "Two halves . . . of the same soul? The dark and the light?"

She nodded slowly. "Somehow we were put back together. I have my memories now, but I also have hers. I feel complete—for the first time in, in forever."

"But how did it happen?" he asked.

"I don't know. I knew I was dying. I lay there, trying to will my remaining strength and life force into her, to help save your son. I didn't realize it was possible to will my soul to heal and to rejoin its other half as well."

"This is all just . . . it's so . . ."

"Far-fetched. I know. But it's true. I feel it, Matthew, it's all true. I felt it when I set eyes on her. In a way, she truly was my sister. And a part of me."

She could sense him trying to deal with this knowledge. "So are you Gabriella or are you Puabi?"

She shook her head slowly. "I like to think I was reborn last night. You named me, when you pulled me from the sea. Poppy. That's who I am now."

He smiled gently, stroked her hair and kissed her mouth. "I love you. I love you by any name. Whole and well. You're my wife, you know. Legally, you're my wife. Gabriella Fair-child. And the mother of our son." He looked down quickly. "We need a name for him."

"Gabriel," she said. "After the best part of his mother."

He nodded. "I like it."

The baby released his hold on her breast, and Poppy turned him toward her, resting him against her shoulder and patting his back so he would burp. As she did, he squirmed and the blanket fell away.

Poppy looked down—and went still.

On the baby's right hip, clear as day, was a small, berry-colored birthmark in the shape of a crescent moon. The right side. Not the left, but the right. She had given birth to one of the Light Ones. An Immortal High Witch. Not a Dark One, as she had been. He would never need to kill to sustain his life. He'd received immortality as a gift. And suddenly she knew why Murial had wanted him. His heart must be a powerful one, indeed. He was special. And destined for great things.

"It's a miracle we've been given, Poppy," Matthew said, leaning close, replacing the blanket around the baby.

"Oh, Matthew," she whispered. "It's only just the beginning."

# MAGGIE SHAYNE

"Maggie Shayne dazzles!
She's on her way to the stars."
**—Suzanne Forster**

*Three hundred years ago, the good citizens
of Sanctuary believed there was a
witch in their midst...*

## *ETERNITY*
Her name was Raven St. James, a woman whose
unearthly beauty and beguiling charms inspired
rumors of witchcraft. Now she must try to use her
powers to help the only man who tried to save her
from the hangman's noose.

0-515-12407-9

## *INFINITY*
For five centuries, Immortal High Witch Nicodimus has
been suspended in an eternity of darkness. Now his
one love, Arianna, has discovered a way to bring him
back. But the power that returns Nicodimus to her
arms also summons an ancient enemy.
To fight this dark danger, they must confront the
past—and reclaim infinity.

0-515-12610-1

**Available wherever books are sold or at
penguin.com**

Four supernatural tales of desire from four of the
biggest names in paranormal romance.

# Hot Blooded

"Dark Hunger"
by <u>New York Times</u> bestselling author
**Christine Feehan**

"Awaiting Moonrise"
by <u>New York Times</u> bestselling author
**Maggie Shayne**

"The Night Owl"
by **Emma Holly**

"Seduction's Gift"
by **Angela Knight**

0-515-13696-4

J843

Out of This World

#1 *New York Times* Bestselling Author

# J.D. Robb

## A Lieutenant Eve Dallas Story

*New York Times* Bestselling Author
**Laurell K. Hamilton**
An Anita Blake, Vampire Hunter Tale

*USA Today* Bestselling Authors
**Susan Krinard**
**Maggie Shayne**

From a futuristic cop caught in a crisis of the heart to a smoldering vision of an unusual love triangle, from the hunger for a human touch on an alien planet to a witch's desperate search for the love of one man, these tales of paranormal romance will transport you to a time and a place you've never seen before.

0-515-13109-1

**AVAILABLE WHEREVER BOOKS ARE SOLD OR AT
PENGUIN.COM**

(B506)

Catch all the
# Hot Shots

*Six quick reads from
six of your favorite bestselling authors!*

*Magic in the Wind*
by **Christine Feehan**
**0-425-20863-X**

*Bridal Jitters* by **Jayne Castle**
**0-425-20864-8**

*Midnight in Death* by **J.D. Robb**
**0-425-20881-8**

*Spellbound* by **Nora Roberts**
**0-515-14077-5**

*Dragonswan* by **Sherrilyn Kenyon**
**0-515-14079-1**

*Immortality* by **Maggie Shayne**
**0-515-14078-3**

J864